Literature & Thought

DARK DAYS

AMERICA'S GREAT DEPRESSION

Perfection Learning

EDITORIAL DIRECTOR   Julie A. Schumacher

SENIOR EDITOR   Terry Ofner

EDITOR   Sherrie Voss Matthews

PERMISSIONS   Laura Pieper

REVIEWERS   Laurie Bauer

DESIGN AND PHOTO RESEARCH   William Seabright and Associates,
Wilmette, Illinois

COVER ART   SUNDAY 1926 Edward Hopper
Oil on canvas, 29"x34"

ACKNOWLEDGMENTS

"America on Easy Street" by Gail Stewart, from *The New Deal* (1993). Reprinted by permission of the author.

"Americans Get a New Deal" by Bruce Glassman, from *The Crash of '29 and the New Deal.* Reprinted by permission of Blackbirch Press.

"Brother Can You Spare a Dime," lyrics by E. Y. "Yip" Harburg and Jay Gorney. Published by Glocca Morra Music, administered by Next Decade Entertainment, Inc., and Gorney Music. Reprinted by permission.

"Brother, Can You Spare a Dream?" by Jackie French Koller, copyright © 1999 by Jackie French Koller, from *Time Capsule: Short Stories about Teenagers Throughout the Twentieth Century* by Donald R. Gallo. Used by permission of Dell Publishing, a division of Random House, Inc.

"Built to Last" by Donald Dale Jackson, from *Smithsonian*, December 1994. Reprinted by permission of the author.

"Debts" by Karen Hesse. From *Out of the Dust* by Karen Hesse. Copyright © 1997 by Karen Hesse. Reprinted by permission of Scholastic Inc.

"Depression Days" by Pat Mora. From *Inheritance of Light*. Reprinted by permission of University of North Texas Press.

"Digging In" by Robert J. Hastings. From *A Nickel's Worth of Skim Milk: A Boy's View of the Great Depression* by Robert J. Hastings. © 1986 by the Board of Trustees, Southern Illinois University, reprinted by permission of the publisher.

"General Douglas MacArthur Fires on Americans" by Lee McCardell, *The Baltimore Sun*.

"Just Hanging On" by Milton Meltzer. Reprinted by permission of the National Urban League.

"King of the Hoboes" by Errol Lincoln Uys, from *Riding the Rails: Teenagers on the Move During the Great Depression*. Reprinted by permission of TV Books. CONTINUED ON PAGE 143

© 2000 by Perfection Learning® Corporation
1000 North Second Avenue
P.O. Box 500, Logan, Iowa 51546-0500
Tel: 1-800-831-4190 • Fax: 1-712-644-2392

Paperback ISBN: 0-7891-5224-X

Cover Craft ® ISBN: 0-7807-9661-6

WHAT WAS THE GREAT DEPRESSION?

The question above is the *essential question* that you will consider as you read this book. The literature, activities, and organization of the book will lead you to think critically about this question and to develop a deeper understanding of America's Great Depression.

To help you shape your answer to the broad essential question, you will read and respond to four sections, or clusters. Each cluster addresses a specific question and thinking skill.

CLUSTER ONE How were people affected? **EVALUATE**

CLUSTER TWO What was the New Deal? **SUMMARIZE**

CLUSTER THREE How tough were the times? **ANALYZE**

CLUSTER FOUR Thinking on your own **SYNTHESIZE**

Notice that the final cluster asks you to think independently about your answer to the essential question—*What was the Great Depression?*

Flood victims line up for food and clothing.
PHOTO BY MARGARET BOURKE-WHITE

BROTHER, CAN YOU SPARE A DIME?

They used to tell me I was building a dream, and so I followed the mob,

When there was earth to plow, or guns to bear, I was always there right on the job.

They used to tell me I was building a dream, with peace and glory ahead,

Why should I be standing in line, just waiting for bread?

Once I built a railroad, I made it run, made it race against time.

Once I built a railroad; now it's done. Brother, can you spare a dime?

Once I built a tower, up to the sun, brick, and rivet, and lime;

Once I built a tower, now it's done. Brother, can you spare a dime?

Once in khaki suits, gee we looked swell,

Full of that Yankee Doodly Dum,

Half a million boots went slogging through Hell,

And I was the boy with the drum!

Say, don't you remember, they called me Al; it was Al all the time.

Why don't you remember, I'm your pal? Buddy, can you spare a dime?

Yip Harburg

DARK DAYS

TABLE OF CONTENTS

Charleston contest, 1926

AMERICA ON EASY STREET

GAIL B. STEWART

Although the Great Depression began in 1929, the roots of the trouble go back earlier, to the end of World War I.[1] The war had been a costly one for America, both in terms of money and human life. The United States spent more than $30 billion in the war, and the country had seen thousands of its young men killed in the brutal trench warfare.

Because the war had been so costly, there was a great political backlash against President Woodrow Wilson and his Democratic party. After the war, Americans blamed Wilson for having dragged them into it. When Warren G. Harding, a Republican, ran for president in 1920 promising a "return to normalcy," he was elected hands down.

"Normalcy" meant that the United States would embrace a policy of *isolationism*—thinking more nationally and less globally. No longer would Americans become involved in the world's problems—it made more sense to concentrate on their own. And no longer would American companies seek world markets for their products. Instead, tariffs were enacted that would discourage foreign businesses from selling products in the United States that might compete with American-made goods.

1 **World War I:** 1914–1918

An Easy Transition

Business and industry had become stronger during the war. Factories had been operating nonstop, turning out tanks, airplanes, rifles, and clothing for the soldiers overseas. The years in which the United States fought in the war saw a mass migration of workers from the farms of rural America to the cities. Workers were desperately needed to fill the factories; employment figures were at an all-time high.

But the need for mass production did not lessen after the war. People were eager to buy radios, refrigerators, and electric washing machines. And the factories, still geared up for a high rate of production, made the easy transition to peacetime industry. With the demand for such goods high, people who wanted jobs had little trouble getting them. And because so many people were working, there were lots of people with money to spend. The cycle of earning and spending continued.

Although business as a whole was booming the years after World War I, there was no industry that grew as fast as the automobile industry, still in its infancy in the 1920s. Glass, steel, oil, and gasoline were needed, as well as paved roads, and these needs meant more jobs for American workers. The demand for Model Ts skyrocketed—the number of cars on American roads soared from 7 million in 1919 to 23 million in 1923.

It seemed that by turning its back to the rest of the world and concentrating on itself, America was rapidly becoming stronger. People were more confident. As one historian writes, "With industry booming and most of America employed, a feeling of great optimism swept the country. The 'American dream' seemed to be working."

mass-produced Model T's ready for sale

A High Regard for Business

Before World War I there had been some serious talk of putting stricter controls on big business in America. Scandals, unfair labor practices, and other improper behavior had been reported, and there were many in Congress who had wanted the government to become more closely involved with how businesses were run.

But the war and its aftermath had changed all that. Hadn't industry swung into high gear to produce weapons and war material when the country needed it most? Few could find fault with the way American industry had contributed toward the war effort. Efficient, quality production had continued, too, to meet the rising demands of Americans for the products they wanted. By the 1920s the reputation of business was golden.

Calvin Coolidge, who took over the presidency after Harding died, felt that business was what the strength of America was built upon. "The business of America is business," Coolidge said in 1924. "The man who builds a factory builds a temple; the man who works there worships there."

Calvin Coolidge (left) and Herbert Hoover

If there were warning signs during Coolidge's term of office that the economy was in for trouble, he did not heed them. "If you see ten troubles coming down the road," Coolidge once explained, "you can be sure that nine will run into the ditch before they reach you." Historians say that Coolidge's "don't go looking for problems" attitude was typical of the 1920s. Business was booming, the economy seemed strong, people were confident. Confident, in fact, almost to the point of feeling invincible.

Spend, Borrow, and Spend Some More

In 1928 Coolidge decided not to run for a second term. His secretary of commerce, Herbert Hoover, was elected to the presidency. Hoover shared his predecessors' views on the economy, and American business continued on its upward spiral.

"We have not yet reached the goal, but given a chance to go forward with the policies of the last eight years," said Hoover in

A construction worker on New York's Empire State Building; the Chrysler Building can be seen in the background.

a 1929 speech, "we shall soon, with the help of God, be within sight of the day when poverty will be banished from the nation."

And the way to eliminate poverty, if one could believe the current wisdom, was to spend money, not save it. Advertisers were assuring American families that it was foolish to tighten their belts, that the more they spent the more prosperous they'd be. People were assured that economist Simon Patten was absolutely right when he said, "I tell my students to spend all they have and borrow more and spend that. It is foolish for persons to scrimp and save."

It seemed, in the late 1920s, that Americans were taking Patten's advice. Spending money was fashionable, and the biggest spenders were the most admired. In January 1929 *Time* magazine's Man of the Year was Walter Chrysler. He had just introduced two new cars, the Plymouth and the luxurious DeSoto. In addition, he was building a gigantic new skyscraper in New York. To the American public, Chrysler was the embodiment of prosperity and strength.

A New Kind of Spending

One sure sign of prosperity was to own things—automobiles, big houses, fancy appliances. But what about the people who did not have money for such products? For these people there came a new phenomenon that allowed almost anyone to be a consumer. It was called "installment buying."

The premise for installment buying was simple. A consumer could buy products on credit. By putting a few dollars down and arranging to make regular payments each month, one could buy a new automobile, an electric washing machine, or an expensive coat. "A dollar down and a dollar when they catch you" became a common saying of the times.

The system was extraordinarily popular. Consumers liked it because it allowed them to own expensive things immediately, instead of after years of saving. Store owners liked the system because it moved merchandise quickly, leaving space for new products. And industry liked it because more consumers were buying their products, creating a demand for their factories to turn out more.

Installment buying became the rule rather than the exception as time went by. By 1928 eight out of every ten cars in the United States were bought on credit. "Coming from a rather poor family, I liked the setup," remembers Sam Johnson, a Minnesotan who was a young man in the 1920s. "I could have my new Ford sitting outside the house the very day I wanted it. People could buy a used one for ten dollars, but I wanted a new one. Now, the people on the next block paid cash for theirs, I'm sure of it. But mine was just as shiny, and the motor worked just as good. For all those people knew, I'd paid for mine same as they did."

Playing the Market

The stock market was another way Americans could take advantage of installment buying. For years, businesses had depended on the stock market as a way to raise money. Instead of borrowing money from a bank, they offered stock in their companies to any investor who could come up with the cash. Each share of stock became more valuable, and *dividends*, another word for interest, were paid regularly to the investor, the amount depending on how successful the business had become.

During the administration of Calvin Coolidge, stock market activity had increased greatly. Even though the stock market had always been risky—for of course one could lose his or her money if the business failed—there was a growing confidence that no business could possibly lose money.

Investors pumped millions of dollars into stocks, driving the price of shares higher and higher. Businesses were being injected with all the money they needed, and so their stocks paid high dividends, enticing more people to "play the market."

By the late 1920s, Americans were able to buy stocks the same way they were buying their automobiles—on installment. Stockbrokers, who did the actual buying and selling of stocks for their clients, allowed customers to pay 10 or 15 percent down on stock. This was called "buying on margin." The broker would loan the rest to his client, receiving the balance of his money when the stock increased in value.

Little Cash, Big Hopes

Playing the stock market soon became the most popular activity in America. Everyone who had a few dollars saved wanted a chance to get rich overnight. Newspapers and magazines were full of "get rich quick" stories—common, ordinary people who had become millionaires overnight by buying the right stock.

The number of stockbrokers in America grew—from fewer than 30,000 in 1920 to more than 70,000 by 1929. Originally confined to plush offices in the nicest parts of the largest cities, the brokers now had offices in every town and village in America. Many set up tiny offices near college campuses and in the poorer sections of town, too, for their clients came from all walks of life.

a street-corner stockbroker in New York City

"Shoe-shine boys were buying $100 worth of stock for $8 and $10," reports Anne Schraff in her book *The Great Depression and the New Deal*. "Stocks were rising in value so fast that 'becoming as rich as Rockefeller' seemed within the grasp of ordinary people. Teenage typists and stenographers, small shopkeepers, and the retired joined the mad buying spree."

It was as if Americans felt that they had a duty to become wealthy. Indeed, those who did not choose to risk money in the stock market were looked upon almost with disdain. Money was there to be made, it seemed, and if one followed a few basic rules, it was childishly simple.

"If a man saves $15 a week and invests in good common stocks," advised John Raskob, Democratic party chairman in the summer of 1929, "and allows the dividends and rights to accumulate, at the end of 20 years he will have at least $80,000 and an income from investments of around $400 a month. He will be rich. And because income can do that, I am firm in my belief that anyone not only can be rich, but ought to be rich."

Warning Signs

Stock prices continued to skyrocket late in 1929, climbing to record heights each week. On the surface this seemed to indicate continued prosperity and growth, but some economists were concerned. Prices had been driven so high, and there was so much investment, that there was nowhere for things to go but downhill.

Especially troubling to experts was the fact that there were so many brokers who had overextended themselves. Record numbers of investors buying on margin had forced brokers to put up large percentages of the money to buy stocks. The stockbrokers were short of cash, so they had borrowed from banks, which were now heavily into debt.

Economists did have one way of controlling the amount of money circulating among banks and stockbrokers. It was the Federal Reserve Board, or Fed, as it is often called. The Fed controls the amount of money in the American economy. It lends money to banks at a rate of interest, just as banks lend money to their customers at a given rate of interest. It is the Fed that determines the rate, for banks and other lending institutions charge their customers the same interest that they themselves are charged.

reading stock quotes from a ticker tape machine

When interest rates are high, it becomes more difficult to borrow large sums of money, because it is so expensive to pay it back. Economists concerned about the furious activity on the stock market decided early in 1927 to use the Fed to cut down on the numbers of stocks bought on margin. They raised the Fed's interest rates. However, there was almost no effect reflected in the market.

In a bolder move later, the Fed declared that money it lent to banks could not be used for investment in the stock market. This ploy seemed to work for a month or so, but eventually prices rose and the upward spiral continued as before.

Sell!

Prices began to drop in the stock market in September 1929. The drop continued all during that month and into October, though many people refused to become alarmed. There had been times before when prices had dropped, but they had always bounced back. However, that was not the case on October 24, known as Black Thursday.

Prices on the stock exchange began dropping crazily all morning. By 11:00 A.M. the plunge was out of control, and the brokers on the floor of the New York Stock Exchange (the nation's largest) were in a state of panic. Anne Schraff describes them as "milling, screaming men, their faces alabaster white with fear."

Prices of what had been good, reliable stocks were half of what they had been the day before. And other investors, noting the plunge, were afraid to sit on their own shares. After all, they thought, by tomorrow the price might be one-fourth of what it had been. They, too, called their brokers and told them to sell. Soon 13 million shares of stock had changed hands.

A reporter from the *New York Times* was present at the New York Stock Exchange that day, and described the terrified investors—thousands of them—throwing their holdings "into the whirling Stock Exchange pit for what they would bring. Losses were tremendous and thousands of prosperous brokerage and bank accounts, sound and healthy a week ago, were completely wrecked in the strange debacle. . . . Wild-eyed speculators crowded the brokerage offices, awed by the disaster which had overtaken many of them."

Panicked stockholders pour out onto Wall Street, October 24, 1929.

Help, But to No Avail

Worried about how so much selling would affect them, some of the nation's most influential bankers hurriedly met that Thursday. They decided to pool $40 million from their banks and buy stock, trying to drive the price up and calm people's fears. The gamble seemed at first as though it would pay off. By the end of Thursday, and again on Friday and Saturday, the market seemed to settle down. However, the following Monday the plunge began again, and this time nothing could stop it.

But Tuesday, October 29, stocks were virtually worthless. On Wall Street, the center for financial activity in New York, there was hysteria, weeping, and even reports of mass suicides among bankers, brokers, and investors. That day, more than 16 million shares of stock were sold. They were put on the market, but no one was buying at any price. Whole fortunes were lost—people who had been among America's richest investors became paupers overnight.

a cartoon from the November 29, 1929 *Wall Street Journal*

Like ripples in a pond, the effects of the crash of the stock market moved outward to include almost every American, investor or not. The Great Depression had begun, and it seemed to be beyond anyone's control.

a 1930's breadline

CONCEPT VOCABULARY

You will find the following terms and definitions useful as you read and discuss the selections in this book.

Alphabet Soup a nickname for the many programs (and their acronyms) President Franklin D. Roosevelt started as a part of the New Deal. Some of the programs were the Agricultural Adjustment Act (AAA), the Civilian Conservation Corps (CCC), the Tennessee Valley Authority (TVA), the Rural Electrification Administration (REA), the Social Security Administration (SSA), and the Works Progress Administration (WPA).

capitalism an economic system based on private or corporate ownership of goods, private control of investments, and competition for goods and services in a free market.

communism an economic system based on communal ownership of all property, government control of investments, and government-controlled distribution of goods and services.

depression a period of low economic activity with high unemployment

foreclosure a legal procedure that ends a buyer's right to pay off the debts on a piece of property; usually caused by the buyer's inability to pay

gold standard an economy where the basic unit of currency is defined by a stated quantity of gold

Hooverville a shantytown of temporary dwellings named after President Herbert Hoover

mortgage A debt against a property. When the debt is paid in full, the mortgage is removed and the property belongs to the buyer.

New Deal The 1932 legislative program of Franklin D. Roosevelt designed to improve the economy during the Great Depression.

recession a period of reduced economic activity

socialism An economic system where goods are owned by the government, and investments and the distribution of goods are determined by the government. Similar to communism.

speculator A person who buys or sells things in order to profit from market fluctuations. A speculator will purchase a baseball card for the sole purpose of selling it at a profit when and if the player becomes a star.

stock certificate a piece of paper showing ownership of one or more shares of a corporation

stock market/stock exchange The place where shares in corporation are bought and sold. Wall Street in New York City is the home of the largest stock exchanges in the U.S.

CLUSTER ONE

How Were People Affected?

Thinking Skill EVALUATING

THE SONG

YIP HARBURG AND STUDS TERKEL

Once in khaki suits,
Gee, we looked swell,
Full of that Yankee Doodle-de-dum
Half a million boots went sloggin' through Hell
I was the kid with the drum,
Say, don't you remember, they called me Al —
It was Al all the time.
Say, don't you remember I'm your pal —
Brother, can you spare a dime.

I never liked the idea of living on scallions[1] in a left bank[2] garret. I like writing in comfort. So I went into business, a classmate and I. I thought I'd retire in a year or two. And a thing called Collapse, bango! socked everything out. 1929. All I had left was a pencil.

Luckily, I had a friend named Ira Gershwin, and he said to me, "You've got your pencil. Get your rhyming dictionary and go to work." I did. There was nothing else to do. I was doing light verse at the time, writing a poem here and there for ten bucks a crack. It was an era when kids at college were interested in light verse and ballads and sonnets. This is the early Thirties.

1 **scallions:** green onions
2 **left bank:** a trendy district of Paris on the left bank of the Seine River

Left: Hundreds of people wait for a free meal in New York City on Christmas Day, 1931.

I was relieved when the Crash came. I was released. Being in business was something I detested. When I found that I could sell a song or a poem, I became me, I became alive. Other people didn't see it that way. They were throwing themselves out of windows.

Someone who lost money found that his life was gone. When I lost my possessions, I found my creativity. I felt I was being born for the first time. So for me the world became beautiful.

With the Crash, I realized that the greatest fantasy of all was business. The only realistic way of making a living was versifying.[3] Living off your imagination.

We thought American business was the Rock of Gibraltar.[4] We were the prosperous nation, and nothing could stop us now. A brownstone house was forever. You gave it to your kids and they put marble fronts on it. There was a feeling of continuity. If you made it, it was there forever. Suddenly the big dream exploded. The impact was unbelievable.

I was walking along the street at that time, and you'd see the bread lines. The biggest one in New York City was owned by William Randolph Hearst. He had a big truck with several people on it, and big cauldrons of hot soup, bread. Fellows with burlap on their shoes were lined up all around Columbus Circle, and went for blocks and blocks around the park, waiting.

There was a skit in one of the first shows I did, *Americana*. This was 1930. In the sketch, Mrs. Ogden Reid of the *Herald Tribune* was very jealous of Hearst's beautiful bread line. It was bigger than her bread line. It was a satiric, volatile show. We needed a song for it.

On stage, we had men in old soldiers' uniforms, dilapidated, waiting around. And then into the song. We had to have a title. And how do you do a song so it isn't maudlin? Not to say: my wife is sick, I've got six children, the Crash put me out of business, hand me a dime. I hate songs of that kind. I hate songs that are on the nose. I don't like songs that describe a historic moment pitifully.

---

3 **versifying:** writing poetry

4 **Rock of Gibraltar:** A stony outcrop on the southern coast of Spain overlooking the passage between the Mediterranean Sea and the Atlantic Ocean. In this instance, the phrase refers to anything thought to be solid.

The prevailing greeting at that time, on every block you passed, by some poor guy coming up, was: "Can you spare a dime?" Or: "Can you spare something for a cup of coffee?" . . . "Brother, Can You Spare a Dime?" finally hit on every block, on every street. I thought that could be a beautiful title. If I could only work it out by telling people, through the song, it isn't just a man asking for a dime.

This is the man who says: I built the railroads. I built that tower. I fought your wars. I was the kid with the drum. Why the hell should I be standing in line now? What happened to all this wealth I created?

I think that's what made the song. Of course, together with the idea and meaning, a song must have poetry. It must have the phrase that rings a bell. The art of song writing is a craft. Yet, "Brother, Can You Spare a Dime?" opens up a political question. Why should this man be penniless at any time in his life, due to some fantastic thing called a Depression or sickness or whatever it is that makes him so insecure?

In the song the man is really saying: I made an investment in this country. Where the hell are my dividends? Is it a dividend to say: "Can you spare a dime?" What the hell is wrong? Let's examine this thing. It's more than just a bit of pathos.[5] It doesn't reduce him to a beggar. It makes him a dignified human, asking questions—and a bit outraged, too, as he should be.

Everybody picked the song up in '30 and '31. Bands were playing it and records were made. When Roosevelt was a candidate for President, the Republicans got pretty worried about it. Some of the network radio people were told to lay low on the song. In some cases, they tried to ban it from the air. But it was too late. The song had already done its damage. ∾

---

5 **pathos:** an expression or artistic representation meant to evoke pity

General Douglas MacArthur Fires on Americans

Lee McCardell

During the summer of 1932 ten thousand veterans of World War I and their families camped outside the Capitol in Washington, D.C. They were petitioning Congress for early payment of their $1,000 bonuses. President Herbert Hoover had refused to meet with the Bonus Expeditionary Force, but did provide them with beds, medicine, and food.

The Senate voted against the veterans, and with nowhere to go, the "Bonus Army" lingered in the camp. Hoover ordered General Douglas MacArthur to remove the veterans "with every kindness and courtesy." MacArthur viewed the men and their families as an unruly mob of Communists. Lee McCardell, a reporter for the Baltimore Sun, was there when MacArthur defied orders and marched the U.S. Army against its own veterans.

July 29, 1932
Washington, D.C.

The Bonus Army was retreating today—in all directions.

Its billets[1] destroyed, its commissary[2] wrecked, its wives and babies misplaced, its leaders lost in the confusion which followed its rout last night by troops of the Regular Army, the former soldiers tramped the streets of Washington and the roads of Maryland and Virginia, foraging for coffee and cigarettes.

. . . The battle really had ended shortly after midnight, when, from the dusty brow of a low hill behind their camp on the Anacostia flats, the rear guard of the Bonus Expeditionary Force fired a final round of Bronx cheers at the tin-hatted infantrymen moving among the flames of Camp Marks.

General Douglas MacArthur (right) prepares to confront the Bonus Army.

The powerful floodlights of Fire Department trucks played over the ruins of the camp. In the shadows behind the trucks four troops of cavalry bivouacked on the bare ground, the reins of their horses hooked under their arms.

The air was still sharply tainted with tear gas.

The fight had begun, as far as the Regular Army was concerned, late yesterday afternoon. The troops had been called out after a veteran of the Bonus Army had been shot and killed by a Washington policeman during a skirmish to drive members of the Bonus Army out of a vacant house on Pennsylvania Avenue, two blocks from the Capitol.

1 **billets:** lodging
2 **commissary:** store for food and supplies

The soldiers numbered between seven hundred and eight hundred men. There was a squadron of the Third Cavalry from Fort Myer, a battalion of the Twelfth Infantry from Fort Washington, and a platoon of tanks (five) from Fort Meade. Most of the police in Washington seemed to be trailing after the soldiers, and traffic was tied up in knots.

The cavalry clattered down Pennsylvania Avenue with drawn sabers.

The infantry came marching along with fixed bayonets.

All Washington smelled a fight, and all Washington turned out to see it.

Streets were jammed with automobiles.

Sidewalks, windows, doorsteps were crowded with people trying to see what was happening.

"Yellow! Yellow!"

From around the ramshackle shelters which they had built on a vacant lot fronting on Pennsylvania Avenue, just above the Capitol, the bedraggled veterans jeered.

And other words less polite.

The cavalrymen stretched out in extended order and rode spectators back on the sidewalks. The infantry started across the lot, bayonets fixed.

Veterans in the rear ranks of a mob that faced the infantry pushed forward. Those in front pushed back. The crowd stuck. An order went down the line of infantrymen. The soldiers stepped back, pulled tear-gas bombs from their belts, and hurled them into the midst of the mob.

Some of the veterans grabbed the bombs and threw them back at the infantry. The exploding tins whizzed around the smooth asphalt like devil chasers, pfutt-pfutt-pfutt. And a gentle southerly wind wafted the gas in the faces of the soldiers and the spectators across the street.

Cavalrymen and infantrymen jerked gas masks out of their haversacks. The spectators, blinded and choking with the unexpected gas attack, broke and fled. Movie photographers who had parked their sound trucks so as to catch a panorama of the skirmish ground away doggedly, tears streaming down their faces.

. . . Veterans with automobiles parked in the jungle behind the mob begin to crank up their machines. Others grab rolls of bedding from their shacks. A tin disk sails through the air down at the west end of the square. Another devil chaser pfutt-pfutts across the surface of the street.

But the breeze is still blowing from the south and the gas drifts back against the attacking party. Newspaper reporters and photographers cut and run for fresh air.

. . . A member of the Bonus Army, somewhat the worse for a serious hangover, finds it difficult to steer a straight course down the middle of one street. He wants to turn.

He argues:

"I don't have to—"

A cavalry saber flashes.

Whack!

"Beat it!"

"I don't have to—"

Whack! Whack!

. . . Somebody got a saber over the head. The men on the truck topple over each other, rolling out into the street.

In a filling station across the way a man—a newspaper reporter— is using a telephone.

"Out of there!" yells the trooper.

The man at the phone hangs on.

The trooper tosses a gas bomb into the station. The man comes out.

. . . Meanwhile the infantrymen have applied the torch. The whole camp goes up in smoke.

The blazing camp sends out a great yellow glow that lights up the sky. The wind freshens and the smoke drifts into the faces of the watching Bonus Army. Motorboats with loud radios come chug-chugging in toward shore to watch the fire.

At half-past twelve General MacArthur returns with Secretary of War Hurley. The dapper Secretary of War is attired in white sport shoes and pants and a flapping felt hat and smokes his cigarette in a debonair fashion. ❧

A One-Woman Crime Wave

Richard Peck

1931

A Great Depression had swept over the nation, and we couldn't seem to throw it off. It was still Hoovering over us, as people said. It hadn't bottomed out yet, but it was heading that way.

You could see hard times from the window of the Wabash Blue Bird. The freight trains on the siding were loaded down with men trying to get from one part of the country to another, looking for work and something to eat. Mary Alice and I watched them as they stood in the open doors of the freight cars. They were walking along the right-of-way too, with nothing in their hands.

Then when we got off the train at Grandma's, a new sign on the platform read:

DRIFTERS KEEP MOVING
THIS MEANS YOU
(SIGNED) O. B. DICKERSON, SHERIFF

But at Grandma's house it seemed to be business as usual. Mary Alice was still skittish about the old snaggletoothed tomcat in the cobhouse. Grandma said if he worried her that much, she ought to use the chamber pot in place of the privy.[1] Chamber pots were under all the beds, and they were handy at night. But Mary Alice wouldn't use hers during the day. She didn't want to climb the stairs just for that. And she didn't want to have to empty it any more than necessary.

---

1 **privy:** outdoor bathroom used before houses had running water

Being nine, Mary Alice decided to take charge. She carried a broom to the privy, to swat the cat if it gave her any trouble. She was soon back that first afternoon, dragging the broom. Her eyes were watering, and she was holding her nose. "Something died in the cobhouse," she said.

"Naw," Grandma said. "It's cheese."

"I don't want any," Mary Alice said.

"It's not for you," Grandma said.

Now that they mentioned it, I could smell something pretty powerful wafting into the kitchen. And I could see the old tomcat from here, stretched out in the yard. He was breathing hard and nowhere near the cobhouse. The cheese smelled bad enough to gas a cat, but it was no use asking what it was for. We were bound to find out.

▲ ▲ ▲

Grandma's house was the last one in town. Next to the row of glads[2] was a woven-wire fence, and on the other side of that a cornfield. On the first nights I'd always lie up in bed, listening to the husky whisper of the dry August corn in the fields. Then on the second night I wouldn't hear anything.

But this year came the sound of shuffling boots and sometimes a voice. The Wabash tracks that cut the town in two ran along the other side of the road. The sheriff's deputies were out, carrying shotguns, moving the drifters along, so they didn't hang around town to beg for food. From my window I watched the swaying lanterns, and ahead of them the slumping figures of the drifters, heading for the next town. It was kind of spooky, and sad.

But it was a short night. At five the next morning Grandma was at the foot of the stairs, banging a spoon against a pan. When we got down to the kitchen, we found her in a pair of men's overalls stuffed into gum boots.[3] She couldn't go outdoors in overalls, so she'd pulled a wash dress on over them, and her apron over that. Crowning it all was her gardening hat. She'd anchored it with a veil to keep the mosquitoes away, and tied it under her chins. She looked like a moving mountain. Mary Alice couldn't believe the overalls.

2 **glads:** gladiolus, types of flowers
3 **gum boots:** rubber boots

"Keeps off the chiggers," Grandma explained. "We're going fishing."

I looked around for the rods and reels, at least some bamboo poles, but didn't see anything.

"It's just one thing after another in town," Grandma declared. "We wasn't over Decoration Day[4] before it was the Fourth of July. Then come the Old Settlers' picnic. You can't hardly get down the street for the crowds, and the dust never settles. I need me a day off and some peace and quiet."

Fresh from the Chicago Loop,[5] Mary Alice and I traded glances.

We didn't linger over breakfast because of the smell. The cheese was on the back porch now, in a gunnysack. It began to dawn on me that it was the kind of cheese catfish consider a delicacy.

Grandma was ready to go, and when she was ready, you'd better be. "Let's get on the road," she said, taking a last look around the kitchen. "Douse the fire and hide the ax and skillet."

We blinked.

"Just a saying," Grandma said. "A country saying. I was a country girl, you know."

She carried the gunnysack of cheese herself, tied to the end of a tree limb hitched up on her shoulder. I was in charge of the picnic hamper, and it took all I had to lift it. I looked inside. Half the hamper was home-canned fruit: tomatoes and pickled peaches. The other half was vegetables from her garden: snap beans, four turnips, a cabbage. The only thing that looked like a picnic was a loaf of unsliced, home-baked bread. But I didn't ask. Grandma saved herself a lot of bother by not being the kind of person you question.

We trooped out into the morning behind her. As soon as we left her yard, we were in the country, but I had the feeling it could be a long trip. The hamper weighed a ton, and I had no luck in getting Mary Alice to carry the other handle.

We were well covered against chiggers, and the day was already too hot. Mary Alice preferred skirts, but she had on her playsuit with the long pants. Being eleven, I was way too old for shorts anyway, so I had on my jeans. We marched behind Grandma, and it wasn't too bad until the sun came up over the tassels on the corn.

We ate the dust of the road for a mile or so. Of course being a city boy,

---

4 **Decoration Day:** another name for Memorial Day. It comes from the tradition of decorating veterans' graves with flowers on that day.

5 **Chicago Loop:** busy downtown district of Chicago

I didn't know what a mile was, but it felt like a mile. At a stand of timber we veered across a pasture.

"Watch your step," Grandma said. "Cow pies aplenty."

We were making for Salt Creek, and pretty soon the trees along the creek began to show on the horizon. But they were like a mirage that keeps its distance.

Finally we came to a barbed-wire fence with a sign on it:

NO TRESPASSING WHATSOEVER
NO FISHING, NOTHIN
PRIVATE PROPERTY
OF
PIATT COUNTY ROD & GUN CLUB
(SIGNED) O. B. DICKERSON, SHERIFF

"Lift that wire so I can skin under," Grandma said.

The lowest wire was pretty close to the ground. But Grandma was already flat on her back in the weeds. She'd pushed the cheese through. Now she began to work her shoulders to inch herself under. I pulled up on the wire to the best of my ability, but there wasn't much slack to it. The barbs snagged her hat, though they cleared her nose. But now here came her bosom. Mary Alice stood by, sucking in her own small chest, hoping to help. The wire cut my hand, and I was stabbed three times by the barbs. But like a miracle, Grandma shimmied under. Mary Alice followed with plenty of room, though she didn't like to get burrs in her hair.

Being a boy, I climbed the wires and pivoted over on a fence post, on the heel of my wounded hand. I dragged the hamper through, and now we were in forbidden territory. It all looked overgrown and deserted to me. But Grandma, speaking low, said, "Hush up from here on, and keep just behind me."

We were in trees and tall grass. As we sloped to the creek bottoms, the ground grew soggy underfoot. Dragonflies skated over the scum on the stagnant backwater. Grandma made her way along the willows weeping into the water. When she pulled back a tangle of vines, we saw an old, worn-out, snub-nosed rowboat. It was pulled up and tied to a tree, and the oars were shipped in the wet bottom, beside a long pole with a steel hook at the end.

"Work that rope loose," Grandma whispered to me. She pointed for Mary Alice to climb aboard, and she followed, reaching back to me for the hamper. The knot was easy, but pushing the boat out with Grandma in it wasn't. By the time the boat was afloat, I was up to my shoetops in muddy water.

I never thought for a minute that this was Grandma's boat. But she was one expert rower. She had the oars in the locks, and they pulled the water with hardly a ripple. She turned us and rowed along the bank, under the low-hanging limbs. We were on our way somewhere, quiet as the morning.

I was in the back of the boat, lolling, my mind drifting. Then I got the scare of my life. A low limb writhed and looped. I caught a quick glimpse of sliding scales and an evil eye, maybe a fang. Then an enormous snake dropped into the boat.

It just missed Grandma's lap and fell hissing between her and me. The last thing I saw was this thing, thick as a tire, snapping into a coil.

▲   ▲   ▲

When I came to, we were tied up to a sapling, and Grandma was crouched over me. She was applying a rag wet with creek water to my forehead. Mary Alice was behind her, looking round-eyed at me.

"You fainted, Joey," she accused.

Boys don't faint. I passed out, and it was probably mostly the heat. Sunstroke maybe. Then I remembered the snake and grabbed up my knees.

"Never mind," Grandma said. "It's gone. It was harmless. Good-sized, but harmless. There's cottonmouths around though, so I'd keep my hands in the boat if I was you."

"It was swell," Mary Alice said. "It was *keen*. You should have seen how Grandma grabbed it up by its tail and snapped it just once and broke its neck."

It was all neck, if you asked me.

"Then she hauled off and flung it way out in the water," Mary Alice went on relentlessly. "Grandma's something with snakes. You should have seen—"

"Okay, okay," I muttered. Grandma stifled a rare smile. I suspected she had no high opinion of the bravery of the male sex, and I hadn't done anything to change her mind. Why wasn't it Mary Alice who'd done the fainting? It bothered me off and on for years.

We were under way again, me keeping a sharp eye on low-hanging limbs. I was recovering from everything but embarrassment, and Grandma was rowing out from the bank. Now she was putting up the oars and standing in the boat. It rocked dangerously, though she planted her big boots as wide as the sides allowed. She reached down for the long rod with the hook at the end.

Glancing briefly into the brown water, she plunged the rod into the creek. It hit something, and she began to pull the rod back up, hand over hand. She was weaving to keep her balance in the tipping boat. I wanted to hang on to the sides, but pictured a cottonmouth rearing up and sinking fangs in my hand.

Something broke the surface of the creek, something on a chain Grandma had hooked. It was bigger than the picnic hamper and looked like an orange crate, streaming water. And inside: whipping tails and general writhing.

I thought of cottonmouths and ducked. But they were catfish, mad as hornets, who'd been drawn by Grandma's terrible cheese. She heaved in the crate and unlatched the top. In the bottom of the boat was a wire-and-net contraption that expanded as she filled it with wiggling fish. A catfish is the ugliest thing with gills, and even Mary Alice drew back her feet. Grandma kept at it, bent double in the boat. She was as busy as a bird dog, one of her own favorite sayings. When all the catfish were in the net, flopping their last in the bottom of the boat, she took the new cheese out of the gunnysack and stuck it in the crate.

"Grandma, how did you remember where it was?" I said, amazed. "You couldn't see it, but you snagged it with the hook right off."

"Remembered where I'd sunk it," she said briefly. Now she was lowering the empty crate, baited with cheese, back in the water. Except it wasn't a crate. It was a fish trap. Where we went in Wisconsin to fish, using a fish trap carried a five-dollar fine.

"Grandma," I said, "is trapping fish legal in this state?"

"If it was," she said, "we wouldn't have to be so quiet."

"What's the fine?"

"Nothin' if you don't get caught," she said. "Anyhow, it's not my boat." Which was an example of the way Grandma reasoned. "Them critters love that cheese," she said fondly as the trap sank from view. She bent over the side to try to wash the smell off her hands, nearly swamping the boat.

Soon we were gliding gently downstream, Grandma rowing easy. The catfish were at her feet, flopping less now.

My brain buzzed. Dad was a dedicated fisherman. He tied his own flies.[6] He was a member of the Conservation Club. What if he knew his own mother ran illegal fish traps? Brewing home beer was one thing, because the Prohibition law[7] only profited the bootleggers. But we're talking about good sportsmanship here.

I noticed Mary Alice's eyes on me. She was watching me around Grandma's rowing arm, and she was reading my mind. It was then we decided never to tell Dad.

▲ ▲ ▲

You could say one thing for Grandma's method. You got all your fishing done at once. It wasn't later than eight o'clock, and maybe we'd gotten away with it. It seemed to me we ought to have brought some poles along, and a can of worms, considering our catch. But I thought maybe things would settle down now, and we could have the quiet day in the country Grandma wanted. Then we heard singing.

I almost jumped out of the boat. It had felt as if we three were alone in the world. Now this singing warbled up from around a bend in the creek, like a bad barbershop quartet with extra voices chiming in:

Camptown ladies sing this song,
Doo-dah, doo-dah. . . .

Grandma nudged the boat into the bank just where the creek began to bend. Through the undergrowth we saw a ramshackle building on the far bank. Above the porch was a sign, a plank with words burned in:

ROD & GUN CLUB

A row of empty whisky bottles stood on the porch rail and from behind them came the singing:

Bet my money on the bobtail nag,
Somebody bet on the bay.

The porch sagged with singers—grown men in their underwear, still partying from last night. Old guys in real droopy underwear. It was a grisly sight, and Mary Alice's eyes bugged. I wasn't sure she ought to be seeing this. They were waving bottles and trying to dance. I didn't know what they'd do next. Grandma was fascinated.

---

6 **tied his own flies:** created a fishing lure from feathers, fur, and string

7 **Prohibition law:** the sale of alcohol was illegal in the United States from 1919–1933

As we watched, a skinny old guy with a deputy's badge pinned to his long johns stepped forth and was real sick over the rail into the water.

"Earl T. Askew," Grandma muttered, "president of the Chamber of Commerce."

But now a fat old geezer in the droopiest drawers and nothing else pulled himself up on the porch rail. Bottles toppled into the water as he stood barefoot on the rail, teetering back, then forward, while the others behind him roared, "Whoa, whoa."

"Shut up a minute," he roared back at them, "and I'll sing you a *good* song." He took a slug out of the bottle in his fist, and began:

The night that Paddy Murphy died
I never shall forget.
The whole durn town got stinkin' drunk,
And some ain't sober yet.
The only thing they done that night
That filled my heart with fear,
They took the ice right
off the corpse[8]
And put it in the beer.

8 **ice right off the corpse:** before large refrigerators, ice was used to preserve a body before embalming

Then he fell back into the arms of the cheering crowd.

"Ain't that disgusting?" Grandma said. "He couldn't carry a tune in a bucket."

"Who is he?" I whispered.

"O. B. Dickerson, the sheriff," she said, " and them drunk skunks with him is the entire business community of the town."

Mary Alice gasped. The drawers on some of the business community were riding mighty low. "They're not acting right," she said, very prim.

"Men in a bunch never do," Grandma said. They were tight[9] enough to fight too, and we were on their private property. Not only that. We were in a boat full of trapped fish almost under the bloodshot eye of the sheriff. I thought it was time to head upstream as fast as Grandma could row.

But no. She jammed an oar into the bank to push us off. Then she began rowing around the bend. My heart stopped. The full chorus was singing again, louder as were got nearer.

Sweet Adeline, old pal of mine. . . .

The Rod & Gun Club came into view, and so did we. Mary Alice was perched in the bow. Grandma was rowing steady, and I was in the stern, wondering if the fish showed.

It took the drunks on the porch a moment to focus on us. We were sailing right past them now, smooth as silk, big as life.

You're the flower of my heart, Sweet Ad—

They saw us.

And Grandma saw them, as if for the first time. She seemed to lose control of the oars, and her mouth fell open in shock. Mary Alice was already shocked and didn't have to pretend. I didn't know where to look.

Some of the business community were so far gone, they just stared back, unbelieving. They thought they owned this stretch of the creek. A few, seeing that Grandma and Mary Alice were of the opposite sex, scrambled to hide themselves behind the others.

But you never saw anybody looking as scandalized as Grandma was at these old birds in their union suits[10] and less. She was speechless as her gaze passed over them all, recognizing everybody.

It was a silent scene until Sheriff O. B. Dickerson found his voice. "Stop in the name of the law!" he bellowed. "That's my boat!"

9 **tight:** drunk
10 **union suits:** one-piece underwear

Before the Rod & Gun Club was out of sight, Grandma had regained control of the oars. She rowed on as if none of this had ever happened. The sun was beating down, so she didn't push herself. After all, the sheriff couldn't chase us downstream. We were in his boat.

Around another bend and a flock of turtles sunning on stumps, Grandma pulled for the remains of an old dock. We tied up there, and now we were out of the boat, climbing a bluff. Grandma led, dragging the net of catfish. I was in the rear, doing my best with the picnic hamper. Mary Alice was between us, watching where she walked. She was scareder of snakes than she let on, if you ask me.

An old house without a speck of paint on it stood tall on the bluff. Its outbuildings had caved in, and the privy stood at an angle. There were still prairie chickens[11] around in those days, and they were pecking dirt. Otherwise, the place looked lifeless. Rags hung at the windows.

The porch overlooking the creek had fallen off. Grandma tramped around to the far side of the house. She dropped her fish on the ground and waved us inside. Even in full daylight the place looked haunted. I didn't want to go in, but Mary Alice was marching through the door already. So I had to. "Is anybody inside?" I whispered to Grandma as I lugged the hamper past her.

"Nobody but Aunt Puss Chapman," she said, like anybody would know that.

It had been a fine house once. A wide black walnut staircase rose to a landing window with most of its stained glass still in. But it was creepy in here, dim and dusty. Smelled funny too. We went into a room piled up with furniture. Then one of the chairs spoke.

"Where you been, girl?"

Mary Alice flinched, but the old woman lost in the chair was staring straight at Grandma. And calling her *girl*?

She was by many years the oldest person we'd ever seen up till then. Bald as an egg, but she needed a shave. And not a tooth in her head.

"Who's them chilrun with you?" she demanded of Grandma.

"Just kids I found along the crick bank," Grandma said, to our surprise. "They was fishing."

"I don't know as I want them in the house." Aunt Puss Chapman sent us a mean look. "Do they steal?"

"Nothin' you've got," Grandma said, under her breath.

---

11 **prairie chickens:** a bird, similar to a grouse, once commonly found in the Midwest

"Talk up, girl," Aunt Puss said. "You mumble. I've spoken to you about that before." She pulled her shawl closer, though it was the hottest day of the year. "I'm hongry. You hightailed it out of here after breakfast, and I ain't seen hide nor hoof mark of you since."

"She ain't seen me for a week," Grandma mumbled to us. "But she forgets."

Then she called out to Aunt Puss: "Catfish and fried potatoes and onions, vinegar slaw, and a pickled peach apiece. And more of the same for your supper."

"I suppose it beats starving," Aunt Puss snapped. "But hop to it, girl. Stir yer stumps."

I thought I might faint again. Nobody could talk to Grandma like that and live.

She led us back to an old-time kitchen. It was in bad shape, but well stocked: big sacks of potatoes and onions, cornmeal, things in cans. And we'd brought a full hamper to add to Aunt Puss's larder.

I had to fire up the stove with a bunch of kindling while Grandma and Mary Alice went to work on the potatoes and onions. Mary Alice was in as big a daze as I was. "Grandma, is that nasty old lady your aunt?"

I stopped to listen. If she was, that made her our great-great-aunt.

"Naw, I was hired girl to her before I was married," Grandma said. "Lived in this house and fetched and carried for her and slept in the attic."

"You had a room in the attic?"

"Naw, I just slept up there. Had a bed tick with straw in it and changed it every spring. I haven't always lived in the luxury you see me in now."

"What did she pay you, Grandma?"

"Pay? She didn't pay me a plug nickel. But she fed me."

I thought about that.

"And now you feed her," I said, but Grandma didn't reply.

▲　▲　▲

We cleaned the fish on a plank table outdoors. I didn't care much for it. It made me kind of sick to hear Grandma rip the skin off the catfish. She had her own quick way of doing that. But every time, it sounded like the fish screamed. She put me in charge of chopping off their heads, but I didn't like chopping off the head of anything looking back at me. And catfish have mustaches for some reason, which is just plain weird. Finally, Mary Alice took the rusty hatchet out of my hand. And *whomp*, she'd bring down the blade, and that fish head would go flying. Mary Alice was good at it, so I let her do it. Grandma gutted.

It was afternoon before we sat down at the dining-room table under a cobwebby gasolier.[12] Aunt Puss was already at her place, so she was spryer than she looked. Grandma settled at the foot of the table. Without her hat, her white hair hung in damp tendrils. We'd been working like a whole pack of bird dogs.

Watching Aunt Puss gum catfish was not a pretty sight. "These fish taste muddy," she observed. "You'uns catch 'em?"

"Yes," I said.

"No," Mary Alice said.

"What did you use for bait?" Aunt Puss said, looking at both of us.

"Cheese," I said.

"Worms," Mary Alice said, more wisely

Since we couldn't get together on our story, Aunt Puss changed the subject. "You chilrun still in school?"

We nodded.

"Do they whup you?"

"Do they what?" Mary Alice said.

"Do they paddle yer behind when you need it?" Aunt Puss looked interested.

"If they did, I'd quit school," said Mary Alice, who'd just completed third grade.

"They whupped that girl raw." Aunt Puss pointed her fork down the table at Grandma.

I had a sudden thought. Aunt Puss thought Grandma and Mary Alice and I were all about the same age. She hadn't noticed the years passing. That's why Grandma didn't say we were her grandkids. It would just have mixed up Aunt Puss.

"That's when she come to work for me. They'd throwed her out of school." Aunt Puss peered down the table. "Tell 'em why."

We looked at Grandma, naturally interested to know why she'd been throwed—thrown out of school. Grandma waved us away. "I forget," she said.

"I don't!" Aunt Puss waved a fork. "It was because you wadded up

12 **gasolier:** gaslight chandelier

your underdrawers to stop up the flue on the stove and smoke out the schoolhouse. That was the end of yer education!"

"Working for *you* was an education," Grandma muttered, though only Mary Alice and I heard.

▲ ▲ ▲

It took us another hour to clean up the kitchen the way Grandma wanted to leave it. When it was time for us to go, Aunt Puss was back in her chair in the parlor.

"Where do you think you're off to now?" she called out as we trooped through the front hall.

"Down to the sty to slop the hogs," Grandma called back.

"Well, don't dawdle. You dawdle, and I've spoken to you about that before. Get on out of here," Aunt Puss hollered. "Let the door hit you where the dog bit you."

Outdoors I said, "Does she have hogs?"

"She used to," Grandma said. "She was right well-off at one time. She's poor now, but she don't know it."

How could she? She still had her hired girl and plenty to eat.

"You take her food every week, don't you, Grandma?"

"Generally a good big roast chicken. She can gum that for days." Grandma turned down the lane. "It keeps her out of the poor farm, and it gives me a quiet day in the country. That's a fair swap." Then her jaw clenched in its way. "But it's just private business between her and me. And I don't tell my private business."

▲ ▲ ▲

We walked country roads all the way home. Grandma set a brisk pace, and I struggled along behind with a hamper heavy with cleaned catfish. Mary Alice went in the middle, watching where she walked.

By the time we got home, the trees in Grandma's yard were throwing long shadows, and it was evening in her kitchen. Mary Alice and I were both staggering. I was ready to go straight up to bed.

But Grandma said, "Skin down to the cellar and bring up fifteen or twenty bottles of my beer. Just carry two at a time. I don't want any broke."

I whimpered.

But she was turning on Mary Alice. "And you and me's going to fry up a couple pecks of potatoes to go with the fish. There won't be nothing to it. I peeled the potatoes this morning before you two was up."

We stared.

▲   ▲   ▲

The catfish fried in long pans with the potatoes and onions at the other end, popping in the grease. The kitchen was blue with smoke, and night was at the windows before we finished up. "Now get down every platter I own," she told me. Then she sent me for the card table I'd used for my jigsaw puzzle of Charles A. Lindbergh.[13]

Following her lead, we carried everything out into the night, making many trips. We lugged it all across the road and up to the Wabash Railroad right-of-way and planted the card table in the gravel.

Finally, the platters of fish and potatoes overlapped on the table, and the opened beer bottles stood in a row beside the tracks.

As the drifters came along, being hounded out of town, Grandma gave them a good feed and a beer to wet their whistles. Mary Alice helped, in an apron of Grandma's that dragged the ground. They were hollow-eyed men who couldn't believe their luck. Two or three of them, then five or six. Then a bunch, standing around the table, eating with both hands, sharing out the beer. They didn't say much. They didn't thank her. She wasn't looking for thanks.

She'd taken off her overalls and put the same wash dress back on, but she'd tied a fresh apron over it. Her hair was a mess, fanning out

13 **Charles A. Lindbergh:** American pilot and hero. In 1927, he became the first to fly solo across the Atlantic in his plane The Spirit of Saint Louis.

from the bun at the back, white in the moonlight. She watched them feed, working her mouth.

Then we saw the swinging lanterns, the sheriff and his deputies coming along behind to keep the drifters moving.

Up trooped O. B. Dickerson, dressed now with his badge on and his belt full of bullets riding low under his belly. His deputies loomed behind him, but they weren't singing "Sweet Adeline."

"Okay, okay, break it up," he said, elbowing through the drifters. Then he came to Grandma.

"Dagnab it, Mrs. Dowdel, you're everywhere I turn. You're all over me like white on rice. *Now* what do you think you're doing?"

"I'm giving these boys the first eats they've had today."

"Or yesterday," a drifter said.

"Mrs. Dowdel, let me 'splain something to you," the sheriff bawled. "We don't want to feed these loafers. We want 'em out of town."

"They're out of town." Grandma pointed her spatula at the sheriff's feet. "The town stops there. We're in the county."

"Yes, and I'm the sheriff of the county!" O. B. Dickerson bellowed. "You're in my jurisdiction!"

"Do tell," Grandma said. "Run me in."

The minute she said that, all the drifters looked up. That was when Sheriff Dickerson's deputies saw they were outnumbered.

"Mrs. Dowdel," the sheriff boomed, "I wouldn't know what to charge you with first. You're a one-woman crime wave. Where'd you get them fish, for instance?' he said, wisely overlooking the home brews in the drifters' hands.

"Out of a trap in Salt Crick," Grandma remarked. "Same as you get yours."

O. B. Dickerson's eyes bulged. "You accusing me, the sheriff of Piatt County, of running fish traps?" He poked his own chest with a pudgy finger.

"Not this morning," Grandma replied. "You was too drunk."

The drifters chuckled.

"And talkin' about this morning," the sheriff said, his face shading purple even in the darkness, "you stole my boat. That's what we call larceny, Mrs. Dowdel. You could go up for that."

"Oh well, the boat." Grandma made a little gesture with the spatula. "You'll find it tied up at Aunt Puss Chapman's dock. As a rule, I take it back where you tie it up. But of course I couldn't do that this morning. How could I row these grandkids of mine back past the Rod & Gun Club? They'd already seen what no child should—the sheriff and his deputies, blind drunk and naked as jaybirds, dancin' jigs on the porch and I don't know what all. It's like to have marked this girl for life."

Grandma nudged Mary Alice, who stood there in the big apron looking drooped and damaged.

"I'm thinkin' about taking her to the doctor so she can talk it out. I don't want her to develop one of them complexes you hear about."

"Whoa," the deputies murmured behind Sheriff Dickerson.

Earl T. Askew stepped up and said into his ear, "O. B., let's just let sleeping dogs lay. I got my hands full with Mrs. Askew as it is."

The sheriff simmered, but said, "Okay, Earl, if you say so." The sheriff and his posse were in retreat now. But he had to cover himself. "Mrs. Dowdel," he said, pulling a long face, "they's things I can overlook. But it seems to me you're runnin' a soup kitchen without a license from the Board of Health. I have an idea there's a law against that on the books."

"Go look it up, O. B.," Grandma said. "See if there's a law against feeding the hungry. But I have to tell you, you've talked so long, the evidence is all ate up."

And of course it was. The drifters had wolfed down the last morsel. With a small finger, Mary Alice pointed out the bare platters. Only a faint scent of fried catfish lingered on the night air. The empty beer bottles went without saying.

The drifters were moving off down the track, and the deputies were heading back into town. O. B. Dickerson spit in the gravel, swung around, and followed them, his big boots grinding gravel.

We stacked the platters and rounded up the beer bottles for Grandma's next batch. I collapsed the legs on the card table. There wasn't a lot of music in Grandma, but she was humming as we worked, and I thought I recognized the tune:

The night that Paddy Murphy died
I never shall forget. . . .

Then after our quiet day in the country, we carried everything back across the road, under a silver-dollar moon. ∾

King of the Hoboes, Arvel Pearson

Errol Lincoln Uys

Arvel Pearson

As the unemployment lines grew, some people decided their chances for work would be better elsewhere. Men, women, and children hitched free rides on trains to places where they hoped to find work. Arvel Pearson, a veteran hobo of the period, explains that such a means of transportation was not without risks.

The closing of the mines left twelve hundred miners out of work. In six months to a year, people who didn't have a place to raise their own food were practically starving. We were lucky in one respect: My stepfather bought a piece of land and built a house before things got rough.

I was considered a strapping kid, though I weighed around 110 pounds. I heard people talking to my folks and saying things like, "Why should you feed him?" and "Why ain't he out workin'?" I made up my mind I wasn't going to be a burden on anybody, especially my parents.

My mother was apprehensive about my leaving but my stepfather said, "The kid knows his way around. Let him go." He thought I'd come home with my back-end dragging, tired and hungry, but I was determined to make it one way or another.

My first day out, I caught a train at Van Buren, Arkansas. I rode freights all night, and next morning I was in a small town where I had some relatives.

"Any work pickin' strawberries?" I asked them. They said, "There'll be work in a few days."

I worked for fifteen days and made fifty-five cents to two dollars a day, if everything went right. When that job finished, a guy said, "The strawberries will be gettin' ripe in the suburbs of Denver."

A month and a half after I left home, I was in Denver. After Denver, a guy said, "Why don't you try the wheat harvest in Kansas?"

I backtracked a few hundred miles and did some harvesting in Kansas—"You can follow this wheat all the way into the Dakotas, if you want to go with it," I was told. When I finished in Kansas, I caught a train north through Nebraska into Wyoming and the Dakotas.

People advised me to go to California. I'd no desire to go there seeing that 90 percent of the people on the road were headed that way. My greatest ambition was to get to Alaska. I rode the rails to the North. A customs officer came aboard at the border. He asked where I was going. "To Alaska," I said. "You can't get there by train," he told me. A kid from the Ozarks who'd never read much geography didn't know that trains don't go to Alaska. It was twenty-five years before I ever visited Alaska.

▲ ▲ ▲

That's the way I started. I picked up a lot from my stepfather, who was an old-time hobo who'd settled down. As I went along I learned from other experienced hoboes. Let me explain how a hobo caught a freight train back in the 1930s:

When you see the train coming, you start running. When it gets level with you, you reach up with your right hand and grab on at the front of a car. Never catch the rear end 'cause it's liable to swing you in and hurt you, maybe run you over and kill you.

It's the same getting off. You don't swing around like squirrel, but keep one hand holding on tightly. When the train gets to a speed where you can unload, just drop back and hop off. You have to hit the ground running or you could fall and break a leg.

Many times I rode overnight on the top of boxcars. I'd take my belt, pass it under the runner on the catwalk, and hook it through my overalls. With no danger of falling off, I let the train rock me to sleep. I'd also hook myself on with my belt if I was riding on a tanker. It's awful tiresome bouncing up and down all night. You might be holding on with one hand, pretty soon you get sleepy and down you come.

I would never "ride the rods." The old cars had rods under them, where people put boards and lay down. It was dangerous and dusty and once the train gets up speed, you have no way of leaving the rods without rolling off and practically killing yourself. I'd ride the top, I'd ride the engine, I'd even climb onto the caboose. I'd ride anywhere but the rods.

I'd always wait for another train rather than take a chance. I wasn't going to arrive at the harvest fields with one leg off.

Ninety percent of the time I traveled alone. You can travel faster when you don't have to wait on someone else. A couple of times I had a partner but it didn't work out. If you get on a train and your partner doesn't catch it, what are you going to do? If it's not going too fast you can jump off. Otherwise you ride to the next stop and hope that in a day or two he'll get there and you can meet him.

I was a full-fledged hobo in less than two years. I knew enough about railroads to pass as a brakeman, fireman, or engineer. I knew what the different hand signals, whistles, and flags indicated. The old engines had two flags right up front. For example, a red ball on a white background indicated a fast freight—a "red ball" was what you wanted to catch if you were traveling a long distance. You never hopped a local because it stopped everywhere to pick up things like milk cans—you might make fifty miles in a whole day.

Sometimes I put on a striped jacket and a railroad cap and stuck an empty lunch pail on my arm. I had dressed like this and was walking down the tracks at Laramie, Wyoming, when I met a railroad man. "Where ya going?" he asks. "I'm headin' over to Denver," I said. "Come and ride in the caboose with me," he said. All I had to do was make up a little bit of a story.

One winter, I was traveling with a partner, going from Kansas City to Joplin, Missouri. At eleven o'clock at night we went down to the rai-lyards and climbed onto the tender of the Flying Crow, a passenger train going south. We had gone about forty miles when the fireman found us. "OK, you so and sos, if you're gonna ride this train, you're gonna work," he said. We climbed down into the cab. My partner was a husky guy but he'd no experience on trains. The tender was rocking from side to side making it difficult to shovel coal into the firebox.

Three shovels full and my partner had coal all over the cab. The fireman told me to take a turn. I don't think I missed more then two shovels in ten minutes. "Where did you learn to shovel coal, son?" the fireman asked. I told him I'd worked in the coal mines. "I can shovel coal through a ten-inch hole," I said.

▲ ▲ ▲

There were nights I'd get homesick waiting for a train with nobody to talk to, sitting alone on a pile of ties under a water tank out in the middle of nowhere. You're only a kid and you get to dreaming about that warm bed back home and seeing the folks. As long as I was working, my thinking was that if I go back with fifty or one hundred dollars, we'll all be in better shape.

I had a hard time getting a job because I still looked so much like a kid. Matter of fact, I was a kid. I'd walk up to a boss in a coal mine and ask for a job. He'd look me over and frown. "Kid, what do you think you can do?" I had to put a little brass on my face. "Just anything you got in this coal mine," I'd say. The boss would give me a job to make me prove

Hoboes gather around a fire.

myself. 'Course I had enough experience that I figured I could handle it. And I figured I didn't have anything to lose if he fired me. Nine times out of ten, I could do what I said.

I'd be working beside a person who was fifty years old. He was getting two dollars a day but because I was a kid they reckoned I wasn't worth more than a dollar. You're working just as hard and feel put down. Whenever possible, I tried to show them that I could do a man's work and get a man's wages.

My first year out on the road, I went as long as forty-five days without a dime in my pocket. Some people felt sorry for you and fed you, but others said, "Get this blasted kid outta here!"

The hardest thing for me was to tell a person that I was broke and hungry and ask for something to eat, but when you go for days without food, you change your mind pretty quickly. Older hoboes gave me advice on what I had to do. For instance, if you ask a lady to mow a lawn for a handout, make sure that it's a small lawn, not an acre and a half. That's going to take you hours and make you miss your train.

On a summer day in a small town in Kansas, I saw a lady sitting in a rocking chair on her porch, fanning herself with a newspaper and trying to keep cool. The train I was riding stopped a short distance away. I hopped off and walked over and asked if I could do a chore for a meal.

"Son, you can chop me some wood," she said. She pointed to a rain barrel that stood out in her yard. "When you've cut it, throw it in the barrel."

That lady's ax was awful dull. I was out there working and sweating, wiping and chopping for twenty minutes and I had about five or six sticks.

I saw the lady was in her kitchen fixing me a meal. When she wasn't looking, I grabbed the barrel and turned it upside down. I took the sticks and laid them crosswise over it.

The lady came outside. "That's enough, son," she said. "Come and eat."

When I took my last mouthful, I said, "Lady, I think I hear the train whistle, I'd better be going." I jumped off her porch and ran down the tracks. I guess she was frowning on the next hobo that came along.

▲   ▲   ▲

"Let's go to the World's Fair at Chicago," a man says to me in Denver in 1933.

"That's a heck of a long way," I said. "Why should we go there?"

"We can get jobs and see the fair."

He talked me into going to Chicago. Right away I got a job taking care of the elephants with a big shovel and helping to feed and water them. I was paid fifty cents a day and could sleep in the hay.

It was amazing to see people with money to spend, especially families with kids buying ice cream and going on those rides.

"Boy, I sure would like to do that," I said. I had to shovel all that manure and couldn't go out there and play around.

Taking your childhood and going from a very small kid to an adult in a year or two is rough. By this time, I was a teenager, but there I was thinking of the same things as a nine-year-old kid 'cause I'd missed out on all that. Things like that bother you.

▲ ▲ ▲

I'd worked in the Colorado strawberry harvest and saved forty dollars, when I learned my folks were destitute. I rode a freight train back to Arkansas and persuaded them to move to Colorado.

My parents' old beat-up car broke down. I bought bus tickets for my mother and my sister. My stepfather, my nine-year-old half brother Luther, and I traveled the rest of the way by freight train. I would put Luther on my back to catch a train on the run, my stepfather getting on first to help us aboard.

My stepfather and I found jobs at the mines in western Colorado. We worked through the winter but then my mother got itchy feet to return to Arkansas. My stepfather wanted to stay and work in the fields in spring but my mother refused. They were stuck down in Arkansas for four years before they could get out again.

▲ ▲ ▲

I'd heard about the King of the Hoboes but had never been to a convention at Britt, Iowa.[1] There were over three hundred candidates in 1939 and my chances were slim, but each day they screened them down. They tested you on your knowledge of different railroads and what the train signals and whistles meant. When it came down to the wire, I was in the top ten. I was competing against experienced hoboes of fifty and sixty. When they announced I was king, I almost passed out. I guess you could call it an honor though being king of the hoboes is just a title. It doesn't amount to anything.

1 **convention at Britt, Iowa:** an annual hobo convention

▲ ▲ ▲

I thought the Depression was going to go on forever. For six or seven years, it didn't look as though things were getting better. The people in Washington, D.C., said they were, but ask the man on the road. . . . He was hungry and his clothes were ragged and he didn't have a job. He didn't think things were picking up.

You leave home with good intentions and tell your folks you're going to come back a millionaire. You return with your head between your arms. You're broke and dirty and they see right away that you didn't make it. I'd stay a day or two and hit the road again.

I was never so desperate that I wanted to commit suicide but I often felt put down. I realized it would take a while to change things. "I'm going to keep going," I said. "I may not end up a millionaire but some-day I will be able to face people I used to beg for food." If I hadn't had hope I would have starved to death by the time I was seventeen.

In those days if we got a pound of bologna, we thought we were doing great. When I go to the store today, I pass the bologna and move over to the T-bone steaks. People see me driving a Cadillac and ask, "If you were on the road that long, how did you accumulate this?"

The road taught me that if I made a dollar, I had to save some of it. I used to have a ledger where I put down everything to see how I was progressing. During the sixties and seventies I was saving an average of five thousand dollars a year. That doesn't sound like much today but over the years it mounts up. When you get to where you don't owe anybody a dime, that's the best feeling you'll ever have, if you live to be a hundred years old. ॐ

JUST HANGING ON

FROM *OPPORTUNITY MAGAZINE*

The economic boom of the Roaring Twenties was not enjoyed by all. Black sharecroppers in the South and black laborers in the industrial cities had just been getting by. When the Crash came, it was devastating to black families. As businesses collapsed, blacks were usually the first workers laid off. In 1931, about one out of two black workers was out of work as compared to one out of four whites.

This report by the Urban League in 1931 uses firsthand accounts to show the difficulties black Americans faced during the 30s.

. . . The R. family came to New York thirty years ago. Eddie, the oldest son, who is twenty-three, was employed in a paint and supply store up to June, when he was laid off. Margaret, age twenty, lost her job in a hat factory that closed down in September. Two children are in high school and two in elementary school. The rent, $65 per month, is four months in arrears, with eviction threatened. When visited the children had been out of school, as they were without shoes and suitable clothing.

The Fords have seven children and expect another in March. Since eviction in October they have occupied one room in a cold water flat, depending wholly on the generosity of neighbors for support. When visited they were without food or fuel. Mr. F. wept like a child when he told the visitor that Mrs. Ford with the baby was at a neighbor's house to keep warm. The entire family invariably slept with their clothes on as there was little or no bedding. Newspapers were frequently placed over the children at night.

Two of the children have been given away and the rest have been "farmed out" to neighbors.

T.J. had resolved to "end the whole damned business." And so when he arrived at the investigator's desk, it wasn't a job he wanted, but a loan of fifty cents. With difficulty the interviewer drew out of him that this was to be spent for a bottle of bi-chloride of mercury.[1] Finally, after being supplied with clothing and a job, a clipping was revealed which gave account of a suicide on the preceding day, the victim being the applicant's roommate who, being out of work for ten months and in despondency, had dressed himself in his evening suit, leaving a note saying, "Death can't be any worse than what I have suffered."

But the silent sufferers who, like Aspinards from Louisiana, are "too proud to beg," never find their way into a relief agency. Shivering about an oil stove, with five children sick, they had never accepted charity and had never heard of the relief agencies.

Faith may remove mountains, but it is still "the substance of things hoped for," at least in so far as job seeking goes in the Jenks family. J. has lived with his wife and six children, paying $62 per month rent until May, 1929, when he lost his regular job. The family lived for fourteen years at the same address. When they moved to the present basement, the radio and other furniture were forfeited for back rent. Mr. J., thrifty and righteous, had a substantial savings account which has now been used up. Insurance policies have lapsed. Being a "God fearing" man, he finds it hard to explain his present predicament, having always been taught at the church to which he has been a regular contributor, to "trust in the Lord." He is still praying that he may yet find a job.

G.S., now twenty-two, left college at the age of nineteen because his father was ill, and there being five smaller children, he became the main support. Since coming from Georgia ten years ago, with the mother working, they had saved about $2,000 which was invested in a suburban home in Jamaica,[2] but unemployment hit them almost a year ago. Foreclosure proceedings followed. Not being the "head of the family," he could not qualify for an emergency work job.

Hundreds of persons have during the past few months experienced similar hardships. From ten to twenty eviction cases per day are reported at the Urban League. Fully seventy-five percent of the persons applying for relief are unknown to relief agencies, and up to the past year have never before requested aid. Many have voluntarily given up their homes, pawned their clothes, sold their furniture and are presently hanging only by the barest thread . . . ∾

1 **bi-chloride of mercury:** poison
2 **Jamaica:** a neighborhood in the New York City borough of Queens

RESPONDING TO CLUSTER ONE

HOW WERE PEOPLE AFFECTED?

Thinking Skill EVALUATING

1. The stock market crash of 1929 and the hard times that followed changed people's lives. Think about the people listed in the chart below and **evaluate** their lives before and after the crash.

Name	Life before the crash	Life after the crash
Yip Harburg		
Bonus Army protesters		
Families from "Just Hanging On"		
Arvel Pearson		

2. **Summarize** the causes of the Great Depression according to the introductory essay "America on Easy Street" on pages 9 – 17.

3. Yip Harburg explains that he wrote "Brother, Can You Spare a Dime?" to highlight a social issue he thought was important. Think of a song today that deals with a social issue and explain how this contemporary song addresses the topic at hand.

4. **Evaluate** Lee McCardell's article "General Douglas MacArthur Fires on Americans." Tell whether his report is objective (strictly factual), or biased (expresses a personal opinion).

5. List the laws that Grandma breaks in "A One-Woman Crime Wave." **Evaluate** her behavior and decide whether her actions were justified.

Writing Activity: Evaluating Survival Skills

List and **evaluate** the personal qualities and traits the characters and people in this cluster used to get through the Great Depression. Use your list to write an essay that describes the three most useful qualities that you think are necessary to survive hard times. Feel free to add other traits you think will be helpful.

A Strong Essay

- begins with an explanation of the focus of the paper
- develops a paragraph for each survival trait and provides examples from the text
- ends with a concluding paragraph that summarizes the ideas of the essay

CLUSTER TWO

WHAT WAS THE NEW DEAL?
Thinking Skill SUMMARIZING

AMERICANS GET A "NEW DEAL"

BRUCE GLASSMAN

With the Depression and the daily crises that accompanied it, many people began to realize that drastic change was unavoidable. New philosophies about social justice and reform took hold. Programs to provide better working conditions and more money for labor were being proposed. Social reformers believed they were now in a race against time. If something was not changed soon, America could collapse further into chaos or even, perhaps, into revolution.

Since 1932 was an election year, the logical place to turn was to the Democrats. Leading the party against Hoover's Republican administration was the governor of New York, Franklin Delano Roosevelt.

From the outset of the 1932 campaign, it was clear that there were many differences between Roosevelt and Hoover, in both political thought and personal style. Roosevelt had been born into an old, aristocratic family of New York's Hudson River Valley. Whereas Hoover was a practical, self-made farmer's son from Iowa, Roosevelt had been reared in the ways of *politesse* (quiet decorum) and *noblesse oblige* (the idea that the privileged should act generously and responsibly toward the public). As a popular governor of New York State from 1928–1932, Roosevelt implemented at the state level the belief of fellow "reform Democrats" that government should come to the aid of victims of economic hardship. As early as 1929, the governor's relief programs included aid to farmers, regulation of utilities prices, and pension plans for the elderly. With the deepening of the depression, by 1931 Roosevelt began to hire

Left: Franklin Roosevelt greets a mine worker during a 1932 campaign trip.

The shuttered bank became a terrifying reality for Americans.

as advisers a number of scholars and experts in government and economics. The purpose of this was to begin to design an overall program of social welfare and reform, for it was the governor's strong belief that entirely new programs would be needed to save the American system of private enterprise from collapse. Thus was born the famous "Brain Trust" of the Roosevelt presidency.

Roosevelt was elected president in November, 1932, winning the electoral votes of all but six states. By Inauguration Day, March 4, 1933, more than 15 million employable Americans were out of work. After being sworn in at the inaugural ceremony, Franklin Delano Roosevelt spoke to the nation for the first time as president. Millions of Americans stood eagerly by, awaiting words of encouragement and determination, and the new president delivered one of the most memorable speeches in American history, saying, in part:

"Let me assert my firm belief that the only thing we have to fear is fear itself—nameless, unreasoning, unjustified terror which paralyzes needed efforts to convert retreat into advance. This nation asks for action, and asks for action now."

With these words, a new approach to the problems of economic depression was born.

The task that Roosevelt undertook was enormous. The problem that required his earliest attention was the collapse of the banking system. The majority of the banks in the country had closed, along with the Chicago Grain Exchange and the New York Stock Exchange. Only four hours after his inauguration, Roosevelt called his Secretary of the Treasury, William Woodin, and ordered him to draft emergency legislation relating to the regulation of banks. The following day, two executive orders were issued: The first proclaimed a national "bank holiday," which provided for the closing of the banks that were still open, in order to prevent depositors from withdrawing all their money; the second order prohibited the export of gold. These two swift actions stopped virtually all economic activity and gave the new administration some time to plan action. An emergency session of Congress was called for March 9.

Experts and legislators worked day and night in their efforts to devise a program that would revive the banking system. Finally, a bill was ready. The bill extended government assistance to private banks and gave the president complete control over gold shipments. It also granted the power to issue new currency through the Federal Reserve Banks and placed the failed banks into the hands of the federal government. Thus the government would conduct the orderly reopening of banks that still had sufficient funds left in their vaults.

On Sunday evening, March 12, Americans turned on their radios to hear Roosevelt's first "fireside chat," an informal, friendly address to the nation. Over the airwaves came the encouraging words that America's banks were once

Roosevelt during a fireside chat

again secure and safe for deposits. So powerful and influential was Roosevelt's message that the next day, when the banks reopened their doors, deposits actually exceeded withdrawals. Confidence had been restored.

Even more popular than the first fireside chat was the message sent on March 13, which called for an amendment to the Volstead Act, the bill that made the manufacture and sale of alcohol illegal. The amended act would legalize the sale of beer, and soon after, all alcohol was once again made legal with passage of the Twenty-first Amendment to the Constitution.

For the next few months, Roosevelt's administration undertook a massive program of legislation that was to affect practically all areas of American life. Known since then as the "Hundred Days," this period changed forever the role of government in American society. ๛

BUILT TO LAST

DONALD DALE JACKSON

There were 30 boys from my county in Arkansas who went into the CCC[1] the same day in 1936. We took a train west from Little Rock, and they called our names when we stopped at Clarksville. It was about midnight. They put us on a truck and hauled us to a camp in the woods at the end of a dead-end road, in rugged country. It just worried me. I was 17 and scared of most everything.

"The boys in camp came out in their skivvies hollerin' 'Fresh meat!' They meant us. We were all poor, hardly anybody had been away from home before. Three of the 30 ran off that night and never came back. They issued us two dress uniforms and two work uniforms and two pairs of Army shoes, and that scared me too because it was more clothes than I'd seen before. And they said that if we lost any clothes our parents would have to pay, and I knew mine couldn't."

Wayman Wells, a 75-year-old retired machinist, smiled as he recalled the skittish teenager he was on that long-ago summer midnight he became a member of the Civilian Conservation Corps. But like every other CCC veteran I met on a swing through four states in search of them, he remembered with pride his time in what was arguably the New Deal's most popular agency: "I believe I'd be there yet if they'd-a let me," he allowed.

Wells and the other men whose lives were changed for the better by the experience are one of the great legacies of the program that began at the dawn of Franklin D. Roosevelt's first term in 1933 and persisted

1 **CCC**: Civilian Conservation Corps

until 1942. Another is the work they left behind, a splendid heritage of parks, dams, bridges, buildings, roads, and hundreds of conservation and restoration projects in every corner of the country.

The CCC got out of the blocks[2] with what may be an all-time record for bureaucratic speed. Only 35 days elapsed between FDR's Inauguration and the enrollment of the first CCC boy—they were always called "boys"—on April 7, 1933. In that time, legislation was written, passed and signed, guidelines were set, campsite selection begun and, most remarkable of all, four Cabinet departments—Labor, Interior, Agriculture and War—were harnessed together to run the program. By July there were 274,375 boys in 1,300 camps.

To qualify, a boy had to be between 17 (18 at first) and 25 (28 later on), single, jobless, in good physical condition and needy. He signed up voluntarily at the local relief agency designated as the selection office. He enrolled for a six-month term, which he could extend for up to two years—longer if he was promoted to a leadership job. Five percent of the original 250,000 washed out in the first few months, most for refusing to work or going AWOL.[3] Enrollees were paid $30 a month, $22 to $25 of which was sent home to their families. At its peak, in September 1935, the CCC mustered 502,000 members in 2,514 camps. Overall, 2.9 million served in nine years.

The Army built and ran the camps, which normally included four barracks with 40 to 50 men in each, along with a mess hall, recreation building, officers' quarters, a school for night classes, and a latrine and bathhouse separate from the barracks. The boys got up to a bugler's reveille,[4] stood morning and evening formations, and showed up on time for meals or went hungry. When they trucked or trudged to work each morning, the Army bowed out and, most often, the U.S. Forest Service took over. Civilian foremen and "local experienced men," called LEMS, ran the work crews. Most of the work was manual labor; their tools were shovels and mattocks[5] and sledgehammers, double-edged axes and crosscut saws. The bulk of the CCC's 200,000 black enrollees served in segregated companies. The rules were relaxed for Native Americans and for World War I veterans. The veterans were, of course, older men; and

2 **got out of the blocks:** got started. The idiom comes from foot racing, where sprinters used foot-sized "blocks" to push against to get a fast start.

3 **AWOL:** short for absent without leave

4 **reveille:** a bugle call at sunrise

5 **mattock:** a tool for digging

in the case of the Indians, the tribal council administered the projects, and enrollees were assigned to work in their own communities.

The average CCC enrollee, according to a statistical portrait compiled by the agency, joined at 18 1/2, stayed in for nine months, and gained from 12 to 30 pounds and a half-inch in height during his tour. He had finished the eighth grade, had held no regular job before the CCC, and had three to four family members dependent on his paycheck. Sixty percent were from small towns or farms.

But if the CCC was a lifeline for the undernourished sons of the Depression, it was a boon of another kind for the country at large. CCC veterans have only slowly come to realize that the work they performed to help their families survive produced a national treasure of fine and lasting structures.

The masonry dam and bridge at Cumberland Mountain State Park near Crossville, Tennessee, built with hand-hewn sandstone, is a graceful

bridge at Cumberland Mountain State Park built by the CCC

yet solid edifice reminiscent of a Roman aqueduct.[6] "I've met three old boys who claim they built that dam by themselves," Wayman Wells joked. The red pine log headquarters of the Chippewa National Forest in Cass Lake, Minnesota, one of the largest log buildings anywhere, is a masterpiece of precisely notched and grooved logs. The magnificent amphitheater at Mt. Tamalpais State Park in California, modeled after a Greco-Roman theater in Sicily, contains 5,000 stones weighing more than 600 pounds each. The limestone boathouse at Backbone State Park in Iowa, a delicate building with intricate and playful stonework, stands guard like a miniature castle over a CCC-made, 135-acre lake.

Robert Ritchie, a CCC vet from Hansell, Iowa, who worked at Backbone Park, expressed the late-blooming pride that many veterans share: "I thought of the C's as just a phase in my life, but as you go on, you feel that it, that you, were a part of the country and of history. We have this park; it was wilderness before, and now it's a nice place to go, and I had something to do with that. I was part of an important event."

Life in the CCC, with such niceties as three squares a day, indoor plumbing and electricity, was a step up for many boys from destitute rural families. "It was better than what I was used to," Clinton Boyer of St. Louis said. "At home we had no running water and used oil lamps." Lonnie Goddard of Bradley, West Virginia, recalled making a single egg

CCC workers on a lunch break

6 **Roman aqueduct:** stone structure used to transport water. The Romans built many aqueducts still in use in Europe.

do for two meals on his family's Appalachian farm. "I'd have the white for breakfast and put the yellow on corn bread for lunch at school."

These were boys whose horizons were pinched by poverty. Doyle Jones of Jamestown, Tennessee, recalls every detail about his train ride to CCC camp because he'd never made a trip like that before. "They took us on the Southern Railway to Knoxville and then by the Louisville and Nashville to Chatsworth, Georgia. I recollect it even now because there wasn't much going on in my life at the time." At camp, Jones was startled to find such exotic foods as bananas and oranges on his tray. Jones' family used his $25 monthly allotment to pay off their grocery bill. "Kirby Johnson at the store, he'd just subtract $25 from what they owed."

They remember the food with a fondness born in deprivation. "Oh, they really fed us, especially breakfast," recalled Harry Marsanick of Florissant, Missouri, "ham and potatoes and sausage, all the eggs you wanted. The kitchen was enough to keep me happy."

In 1942, when CCC funding stopped and most of the boys had changed to other uniforms, the agency issued a report summarizing its accomplishments. The numbers on the volume and variety of work were awesome: 46,854 bridges of various kinds built, 3,116 fire-lookout towers, more than 28 million rods[7] of fencing, 318,076 "check dams" for erosion control, 33,087 miles of terracing. CCC lads fought forest fires and mosquitoes and soil erosion, they planted trees and grass, and excavated channels, canals and ditches; they laid pipe and improved wildlife habitat and built or maintained thousands of miles of hiking trails. They did every conservation job that any land manager could think of. And some died: there were accidental drownings and falls; 47 were killed in forest fires; nearly 300 perished when a hurricane flattened three camps of war veterans on the Florida Keys in 1935.

In extremely cold or stormy weather they stayed in camp. "We didn't go out if it was colder than 5 below," Robert Ritchie of Iowa recalled. "We had three weeks like that once. The guys sat around making cigarettes with their machines."

They went to work at 7:15 and quit at 4, with a break for lunch served back at camp or trucked to the site. "They brought lunch in big old kettles, and we'd eat the beans and applesauce all slopped together in our mess kits," Lonnie Goddard remembered. The work was tough. "I filled holes in a road," said Burl Hutchison of Columbus Junction, Iowa. "My station was the business end of a wheelbarrow or shovel. We called the wheelbarrows 'silver streaks' or 'Irish buggies.'" Goddard quarried and

7 **rods:** measure of length, one rod equals 5.5 yards or 5.029 meters

set sandstone. "We'd blast it and then split the rock into smaller chunks with hand tools and load it on trucks with a hand crank." His proudest accomplishment was a stone wall in a state park. "We dug footings and filled them with stone to a depth of 17 feet. Seventeen feet! Do you believe it? And it was beautiful."

The lucky ones learned about craftsmanship. Arthur Jackson, who later owned a successful drilling company in Lebanon, Tennessee, cut blocks of sandstone for the Crossville dam. "It was amazing what the engineers could do with a bunch of ignorant kids," he recalled. "They were patient. They said we were going to do it right, and if you rebelled you got another job. They only wanted boys who were willing to learn."

The CCC boys were civilians, but G.I. discipline governed their camps. "When I first reported, the officers asked me some question and I said 'Yeah,' and they shouted 'What did you mean, Yeah?' " Burl Hutchison of Iowa remembered. "They wanted a 'Yessir,' and I was thinking, 'Oh my, what did I get into?' " "They had a bugle or a whistle for everything," Lonnie Goddard said, "and I was used to roosters and not a bugle waking me up. You made your bunk with six inches of white below the pillow, and everything had to be just so in your foot locker. If you threw your cigarette on the ground you wore a butt can around your neck for a day."

"I laugh whenever I remember that"

Practical jokes were a CCC tradition. New arrivals were dispatched to "water the flagpole." There were dozens of variations on the "snipe hunt": rookies raced off in quest of "striped paint," "bunk spacers," "sky hooks" and other imaginary objects. It was a simpler time: they gleefully short-sheeted one another's beds and tied neatly folded clothing in knots—"that would kind of disappoint you, especially if it was 15 minutes to reveille," said Burl Hutchison.

They concocted their own slang. A cigarette was a "stiffy," its makings, tobacco and paper, were "sawdust and blankets." The officers' orderly, who delivered meals to the brass, was known as "Dog Robber" because he got the choice leftovers the dog might otherwise have enjoyed. If you wanted something at the end of the mess table, Lonnie Goddard remembered, you called out "Butts on the beans!" or whatever it was, and you finagled a drag off another's cigarette by crying "Butts on that cigarette!" In the evenings they played cards or Ping-Pong or music. Guitar picker Doyle Jones joined a band that played for local square dances, while Wayman Wells recollected Arkansas as "harmonica country—those boys could wear a harmonica out."

CCC boys were by and large neither rebels nor troublemakers; they had chosen to be there, and most accepted the discipline and hard work. But from the beginning there were some who did not, and there were occasional uprisings if not full-scale mutinies. Desertion, always a concern, accounted for 11.6 percent of those leaving the corps in 1937, and the percentage increased in later years. A boy was counted a deserter if he was AWOL for eight days. Nobody pursued them, but Harry Dallas of Overland, Missouri, ran into an ex-enrollee 58 years later who was worried that they might still be looking for him. Most deserters left in the first few days, often out of homesickness.

They staged work stoppages and food strikes to protest curfews, cold-weather work and the quantity or quality of the food. In Wayman Wells' Arkansas camp the issue was neckties. "We wore wool uniforms and neckties for retreat review in summer when it was real hot, and they checked to make sure our ties were tight. Well, we called a food strike and nobody ate supper for three days. The doctor got into it, and they finally said we could unbutton the top button of our shirts and wear the tie loose."

The real conflict was not between CCC enrollees and the military but between the boys from the C's and townfolk in nearby communities. Some towns posted "No CCC Allowed" signs. "I think people in general looked down on us," Carl Denoff of Lansing, West Virginia, said. "It was like we were trash, we weren't recognized as equal. But when we'd pass farmhouses on our way to town the girls would holler and wave." On weekends they rode to town, where they sometimes scuffled with the local boys. "That's what bound us together," Lonnie Goddard said. "If the boys in town jumped you they'd have to whip all of us. We were like brothers."

Often enough, the CCC transformed shy, backward country boys who thought of themselves as losers into physically stronger, effective men. Self-esteem, we call it today. "I felt I was going downhill, like the CCC was the bottom of the barrel," said Robert Ritchie, "but I wasn't alone, and I came out positive, more positive as time passed." "I was scared to death of everything," Arthur Jackson of Tennessee recalled. "Just timid. I didn't think I could talk to people. I'd only gone to third grade. The C's gave me confidence that I was as good as anybody. It made me know I could do things, gave me some push. I'm proud that I worked on that Crossville dam. I wasn't afraid to tackle anything after that." ❧

Brother, Can You Spare a Dream?

JACKIE FRENCH KOLLER

Lisa Bridges, English 12, Amherst High School
Oral History Project: The Great Depression
Subject: Samuel Fowler, age 80, Amherst, MA
Visit #3—April 19, 2000

It was a mild spring day when I stopped in for my third visit with Sam Fowler. We sat in the kitchen of his small farmhouse in Amherst and he made us both a cup of tea. Sam has Parkinson's disease, which makes his hands tremble and causes him to move with a slow, shuffling step. His mind is sharp, though, and he still manages to look after his house and care for himself. He has a raspy voice and an old-time Yankee accent. Sam and I spent my first two visits getting to know each other, and by the third, we were on a first-name basis despite the difference in our ages. Sam often talked about missing his wife, May, who had died two years earlier, and I think he had come to look forward to my visits. I felt it was time to press forward with the project.

"As you know, Sam," I said, "I'm studying the Great Depression. Would you mind telling me in your own words what it was like for you?"

Sam rubbed his white-whiskered chin a moment, then sat back in his chair. "Well," he said, "I lived in the Swift River Valley then, y'know, and for us the Depression come early. Boston was outgrowin' her water supply, y'see, and lookin' for someplace to plant a new reservoir, and before you know it there were rumors about the valley. It had everything Boston was lookin' for—plenty of water, a perfect bowl shape, and all it needed were two small dams at its southern end to turn it into a reservoir big enough for Boston to drown in.

"Valley folks thought the rumors were just nonsense at first. Boston was sixty-five miles away, don't forget. But the rumors kept up, and then surveyor's stakes were found in places where they had no business bein', and at last, on a mornin' in 1919, the valley folks picked up their newspapers and read, 'Swift River Doomed!'

"Well, that was the beginnin' of the end. Property values fell, and businesses packed up and left. People started leavin', too, but lots of 'em, like my folks, found themselves trapped in homes that wouldn't sell. When the Swift River Act finally passed in the late twenties, the Metropolitan District Water Supply Commission began buyin' up the properties, but the values had fallen so by then that many folks could hardly pay off their mortgages with the money they got. It was the beginnin' of the Depression and folks had nowhere to turn, so the commission decided to let them lease back their properties and stay on until the dams were built."

"Is that what your folks did?" I asked.

"Yep," said Sam. "The leases they offered were dirt cheap. We got our farm, includin' outbuildings and eighty acres of land, for five dollars a month. That's how we managed to keep our family together and ride out the worst of the Depression."

"Tell me a little about your life in those days," I asked him.

Sam took a sip of his tea, gripping the cup with both hands. "Oh, we were poor. We had no 'lectricity, runnin' water, phone . . . no nothing. And our clothes were patched, and patched, and patched some more. When we outgrew 'em, my ma would cut down somethin' of hers for my younger sister, Kate, or somethin' of Pa's for me. Or sometimes she'd get hand-me-downs from a neighbor or the church, and then she'd make 'em over to fit us.

"Bein' farmers, we always had food, though. We had a milk cow and a coupla chickens, and Pa grew corn and tomatas, pumpkins and beans. We had blueberry bushes and apple trees, so there were always pies 'n' cobblers, and come spring we'd tap the maple trees and make maple-sugar candy. That was our favorite. We had plenty to keep us busy, too—fields to roam, and berries to pick, brooks to splash in and trees to climb. And we had community. Do you know what I mean b'that?"

I shrugged.

Sam sighed, like he'd expected as much. "You young folks today don't know what you're missin'," he said. "We were such a small town, y'see, that everybody knew everybody. We had hay rides and sleigh rides, birthday parties, huskin' bees, town picnics, church suppers . . . And we kids went to everything, even the grange hall dances, which we loved, because the grown-ups always got tipsy, don't you know, and we'd sneak around taking sips out of their glasses when they weren't lookin'." Sam chuckled at the memory.

"Then we'd all dance," he went on, "or more like it—trip over each other's feet—to all the old big-band tunes. Now that was music— Tommy Dorsey, Glenn Miller[1]. . . I remember the 'Beer Barrel Polka' come out 'round that time, and that was a big favorite. Didn't we tear up the floor to that one!"

"It seems that the Depression didn't have too bad an effect on you, then," I said.

"Well, when we got to be teenagers, it was differ'nt, of course. We went up to the high school in Athol then, and we started to care how we looked, you know? Kate got into readin' those movie-star magazines, and natur'ly she wanted to be glamorous like Greta Garbo or Marlene Dietrich.[2] And I started noticin' girls. I remember one day I was walkin' down Main Street and a girl called out my name. I think I was about sixteen at the time. Well, I turned around, and wasn't it Emma Bradley! What a pretty little thing she was. . . ."

Sam looked at me. "I hope you don't take offense at that, me callin' her a pretty little thing. I know young women these days take offense at that sort of thing sometimes. I don't know why. Times are changing so's I hardly understand 'em anymore."

I smiled. "No offense taken, Sam. Go on."

"Well, she was about the prettiest girl in the eleventh grade—cute little figure, and eyes as green as apples in July. I was so surprised to hear her call my name that I turned clear around to see if maybe there wasn't some other Sam standin' behind me."

"Sam," I said with a laugh, "give yourself credit."

Sam laughed. "Oh, I wasn't much to look at. I'm sure she was just bein' neighborly, callin' my name like that. But you know how young boys are. I took it for a sign that maybe she was sweet on me, and that was it. I was smitten. I spent the rest of that school year moonin' over

---

1 **Tommy Dorsey, Glenn Miller:** popular big band leaders of the 1930s

2 **Greta Garbo or Marlene Dietrich:** Hollywood actresses of the 1930s

her. I'd try to second-guess where she was gonna be next so I could be there first, you know? I'd toss a ball against the wall or pretend to be readin' a book, just hopin' she'd call my name again. But she never did. And that's when I b'gan to realize how nice it would be to have a little money.

"See, there were boys in town that did have money. They were the sons of the engineers and construction workers that'd moved to the valley to work on the dams. I remember this one fella, Tommy Cruthers. He took Emma into Athol to see *Les Misérables*. That was the big picture that year. Then there was this other fella, Dennis somethin' er other. He had enough money to buy a Monopoly game. Monopoly was brand-new back then, you know, and everybody was talkin' about it. Well, of course he bought it and invited Emma over to play, and didn't she go on and on about it in school the next day and let Dennis walk her home.

"And then I remember another lad. I think his name was Michaels. Uh . . . David, yes, David Michaels. Well, he went out and bought a copy of *Gone with the Wind*, which had just come out and was all the rage, and he would sit with Emma on a park bench after school and read it to her. If you could see how she used to look into his eyes while he was readin' . . . Well, it near broke my heart, of course, stuck on her the way I was, and I began to scheme how I could get some money, too, so's I could take Emma out and show her a good time."

"Did you have any luck?" I asked.

"Well," said Sam, "the funny thing was, b'fore long an announcement showed up in the local paper. It said that three thousand men were to be hired over the summer to begin clearin' the reservoir basin of brush and trees, and they were to be paid four dollars a day. Now, I'll tell you, four dollars a day was a fortune! My whole family was lucky if we could scrape together four dollars in a *week*. Well, I made up my mind right then and there that I was gonna be first in line when that employment office opened, believe you me.

"Only the employment office never opened—not for us valley folks, anyway. Instead, we got word that Governor Curley was handing out the jobs to Boston men, and that these woodpeckers, as we soon nicknamed them, were to be bused into the valley for the summer. Valley folks were being asked to put 'em up in return for a few dollars' room and board. Well, I don't mind tellin' you I was sore as a wet hen.

"'That ain't fair!' I remember complainin' to my parents. 'We're not gonna take in any of them woodpeckers, are we?'

"'Three dollars a week is better than none,' my ma said. And that was that. Next thing I knew, one of them woodpeckers come knockin' on our door. That's quite an interestin' story, actually. I remember it like yesterday."

Sam paused and looked at me. "That's the funny thing about getting old. Somethin' happened fifty years ago, you remember so clear, and somethin' happened only yesterday . . . Well, never mind.

"Like I was sayin', I come in for supper one night, and the whole kitchen smelled like Ma's maple baked beans. You could always tell summer was on the way when Ma started bakin' beans. She and Kate made extra money peddlin' them off the back of our truck every summer to the folks up on Greenwich Lake.

"Anyway, a knock come on the door this night, and there stood this city slicker with a lumpy old satchel in one hand. He was short and thin, dressed kind of shabby—but then, I was one to talk—and he coulda used a shave and a haircut. He reached out a hand to me. 'Name's Mike McGovern,' he said. 'I'm—'

"'Know who you are,' I told him, and I ignored his hand. That wasn't very polite, I know. But the way I saw it, this fella had stole my job, and I was pretty burned up about it.

"Ma come bustling over and welcomed him in. 'Kate,' she said, 'set another place for our guest.'

"'*Guest?*' I said, givin' the woodpecker a dirty look. 'I thought he was a *boarder*.'

"Well, Ma shot me a look fit to kill, and I knew I'd better mind my manners. As I recall, Kate was pretty mad at me, too. 'Don't mind him none,' she told the woodpecker. 'He's just ignorant.'

"Well, she and I went at it a little bit, the way kids do, till my pa walked in. One look at his face told us he was in no mood for shenanigans.

"'Something wrong?' Ma asked him.

"'The tractor,' Pa muttered. 'Starter's gone.'

"'Oh, dear,' said Ma.

"Everyone was quiet for a moment, and then the woodpecker stepped forward. 'Mike McGovern, sir,' he said, putting out his hand. 'Folks call me Mac. I guess I'll be boardin' with you awhile.'

"I don't think Pa had noticed him till then, and he looked a little embarrassed. He didn't like outsiders to know our troubles. But he played over it. 'Welcome, Mac,' he said, shaking the woodpecker's hand. 'Sit down, please.'

"Pa took his usual seat at the head of the table and offered grace. Mac folded his hands in front of him, and I couldn't help but notice how soft and smooth they were. I doubted he'd ever swung an ax in his life.

"Ma started passing around the platters of food, and Mac filled his plate and dug in like a half-starved cur.[3] I didn't do much talkin', but Ma and Pa and Kate chatted with Mac as they ate. The conversation eventually come 'round to the reservoir.

"'How do folks around here feel about the whole thing?' Mac asked.

"'How do *you* think?' I grumbled.

"Kate gave me a sharp look, then smiled at Mac. 'I, for one, can't *wait* to leave,' she said. 'The valley has gotten so dull. We don't even have our own picture show anymore.'

"Pa cleared his throat. 'Most of us don't see it quite like Kate does,' he told Mac. 'Truth is, we're angry. This valley's our home. Been home to some for generations. We feel we got a raw deal.'

"'Yeah,' I added, 'and we're still gettin' it. They promised us jobs, and instead they go out and bring you city slickers in.'

"There was an awkward silence, and then Mac turned to me. 'I'm sorry about that,' he said, 'but it's not my doin'. The job was offered, and I took it. Reckon you'da done the same.'

"He was right, of course. I would've done exactly the same. But that didn't make me like him or the whole situation one bit better.

"'Enough about us,' Ma said, frowning at me. 'Why don't you tell us about yourself, Mac?'

"Mac paused with a forkful of beans halfway to his mouth.

"'Ain't much to tell,' he said.

"'How about your family?' asked Ma.

"'Got none,' said Mac.

"'Oh, I'm sorry,' said Ma. 'You live with friends, then?'

"Mac shook his head. 'No, ma'am,' he said. 'I'm on my own.'

"Kate's eyes lit up at that. 'Keen,' she said.

"Mac glanced at her. 'Being on your own ain't all it's cracked up to be,' he told her. 'I wouldn't be in such a big hurry for it if I were you.'

"Kate colored up. 'You would if you lived in *this* town,' she mumbled.

"'If you don't mind my asking,' said Ma, 'how old are you, Mac?'

"'Seventeen. Just graduated twelfth grade.'

"'Ever done land clearin' before?' Pa asked.

3 **cur:** dog

"Mac laughed. 'I'm afraid there's not much uncleared land in Boston,' he said. 'I've run errands, shined shoes, peddled papers, hauled ice—earned a buck just about any way I could. Last few years it's been tough, though. Grown men'll fight you for any job these days.'

"'Still,' said Kate, 'it must be so excitin' to live in a big city. I'll bet there's a picture show on every corner. Hey! Maybe I can come visit you when you get back.'

"Ma just about dropped her teeth at that. 'Kathleen Fowler, I declare!' she cried.

"'Don't worry,' Mac told her. 'I'm not *goin'* back. Soon as this job's done I'm heading to Ohio. Got me a scholarship to college out there.'

"'Hotsy totsy!' said Kate. 'A college man!'

"Well, that did it. Ma plunked her glass down on the table, sloshing water all over the place. 'Kathleen Fowler!' she said. 'To your room. Now!'

"Well, Kate jumped up and put on a big show of falling on her knees by Ma's chair and beggin' forgiveness. She always was dramatic like that, and being the youngest, and a girl, she could get away with just about anything. Next thing you know, Pa was chucklin' into his napkin and Ma was throwing her hands up.

"'Oh, very well,' she told Kate. 'Mind your manners and help me get dessert.'

"'I really do think it's the bee's knees that you're going to college,' Kate told Mac when she slid back into her chair. 'I'm such a dumb Dora, I'll be lucky if I get through high school. Latin positively gives me fits.'

"Mac smiled. 'Readin' and writin' just come easy to me,' he said. 'I figure college is my ticket out of—' He stopped speaking then, and turned red. I reckon he realized he'd put his foot in his mouth. 'Anyhow, that's why I need this job,' he added quickly. 'To pay my way to Ohio and buy my books.' He finished his pie then and made a show of yawning. 'If you all don't mind,' he said, 'it's been a long day. . . .'

"'Oh, certainly,' Ma nodded at me. 'Go along and show Mac where he'll be staying, Sam,' she said.

"'But I'm not done with my pie,' I told her.

"'I'll take him,' said Kate, jumping up.

"Ma put a hand on Kate's arm and gave me a hard look. 'Sam will take him,' she said. 'Won't you, Sam?'

"'Yes, ma'am,' I said, but I shoveled the last of my pie into my mouth before I got up."

I asked Sam, "Did Mac stay in the house with your family?"

"Yep," he answered. "Stayed in my room, in fact. I had twin beds, you know, and Ma had cleared out a dresser for him. I remember watchin' as he unpacked his things. He had a few items of clothing and he put those in his top drawer, but mostly what he had was a bunch of beat-up old books. And didn't he treat them like gold, liftin' them out one by one and arranging them on the dresser top.

"'What're all them books for?' I asked him.

"'Readin',' he said.

"'That's a lot of readin',' I told him. 'Must be nice to have that kind of free time.'

"Well, I was just givin' him a hard time, of course, and he knew it, so he didn't answer, which made me all the angrier.

"'Oh, I forgot,' I said sarcastically. 'Reading is your ticket out of this Depression, ain't it? Must be nice to have one of them tickets. I thought I had one, too. It was called a job. But they gave it to—'

"'Look,' Mac interrupted, 'I told you I'm sorry about that, but it's not my doing. Now, if you'll just show me where the bathroom is . . .'

"I laughed. 'You'll find it in the backyard,' I told him, 'only we call it a privy. Welcome to the country, city boy.'"

"So they would have had plumbing in the cities back then?" I inquired.

"Oh, sure," said Sam. "That was the mid-thirties. They had plumbing, 'lectricity, everything."

"So Mac was really roughing it living with you?"

Sam chuckled to himself. "Yep. But he was no baby. In fact, I was up at the first cock's crow that next morning, and wasn't that son of a gun's bed empty already! That caught me by surprise, to tell the truth, but I remember thinking to myself, We'll just see if he's such an eager beaver after his first day of real labor.

"Sure enough, he dragged in that evening lookin' worse than a whipped dog. His hands were so blistered that his work gloves were soaked with blood. His face and neck were covered with bug bites. His clothes were all snagged and torn, and the sole of one of his shoes was loose and flapping. He was a mess, all right.

"'You poor boy,' Ma fretted. 'Go douse yourself at the pump with some nice cool water, then come in and let me tend to those blisters.'

"I have to admit I was gloating a little to myself. At that rate I was sure he wouldn't last another day. He did, though, son of a gun. Next morning he tied his shoe up with an old rag, rubbed a little more of Ma's bag balm into his blisters, and trudged off without a complaint. By the end of the week I had to admit he'd earned my respect. I figured anybody that worked that hard couldn't be all bad. I dug an old pair of boots out of a box in the barn and cleaned the dirt and mildew off of them as best I could.

"'Here,' I said when he got home that night. 'Your feet look a little smaller than mine. If these fit, you can have 'em.'

"Well, he wanted them all right. That was plain. But he didn't reach for 'em right away. Pride held him back, I s'pose.

"'Boots were just rotting out there in the barn,' I told him. 'Ain't no big deal.'

"He hesitated a little longer, then he swallowed his pride and sat right down and pulled 'em on. They seemed to fit fair enough. He looked up and gave me an embarrassed smile. ''Preciate it,' he said quietly.

"I nodded and walked away. No use makin' him feel any worse, you know?"

"That was really nice of you," I said.

Sam looked down. "Just common decency is all," he muttered; then he took another sip of tea.

"That must be cold," I said. "Can I heat it up for you?"

"No, no," said Sam. "I don't much like tea, t'be honest. It's just somethin' to sip. May used to make a good pot of coffee, and I liked that. My doctor won't let me have coffee no more, though." He shook his head. "Terrible thing, getting old." He looked over at the stove and seemed to drift off.

"Sam?" I said after a while.

"Yep?" He looked back at me and blushed. "Sorry. Mind wanders sometimes, y'know. Where was I now? Oh, yes, that woodpecker fella. Well, it was about a week after I give him the boots that Pa come hur-ryin' toward me across the cornfield one day. Even at that distance I could tell somethin' was wrong.

"'Milk wagon stopped by with bad news,' he told me. 'Mac's been hurt. They got him down to Doc Segur's. Tree fell on him. Busted up his leg pretty bad.'

"I winced. 'Those fool woodpeckers,' I said. 'Be lucky if they don't all kill each other. How bad is he?'

"'Bone's shattered,' Pa said. 'Doc patched him up, but he's gonna be laid up for some time. You better take the truck down and bring him home.'

"Now, I'm not proud to tell you this, but soon as I heard that he was gonna be laid up awhile, my ears perked up.

"'Laid up?' I said to Pa. 'How long?'

"Pa scratched his head. 'Coupla months, I'll wager.'

"'His job'll be open, then,' I said quietly.

"Pa stared at me, chewing on my meaning, and I could see he didn't much like the taste.

"'If I don't go after it,' I told him, 'someone else will.'

"Pa sighed and nodded. 'Seems a damn lousy thing to do,' he said, 'but you got a point, son. Guess you ought to stop by the commission on your way to the doc's.'

"It was hard telling Mac I'd gotten his job. He laid in his bed there, with his cast propped up on a coupla books, and he just stared at me.

"'If I didn't go after it, someone else would've,' I told him.

"He dropped his eyes. 'Ain't blaming you,' he said. 'I'da done the same thing.' Then he turned his face to the wall.

"Well, I felt bad for him, but I forgot about it pretty quick when I got my first week's pay. I give half of it to Ma, then I spent the rest on a box of Fannie Farmer chocolates, two tickets to the Fireman's Ball, a bottle of hair tonic, and a new shirt. I rubbed the tonic into my scalp, slicked back my hair, put on the shirt, stuck the tickets in my pocket and the candy under my arm, and marched across town and right up to Emma Bradley's front porch.

"She looked mighty surprised to see me. 'Why, Sam,' she said when I handed her the candy. 'Is this for me?'

"'Yep,' I told her.

"'Well, aren't you just the sweetest thing,' she said. Then she stretched right up there on her tiptoes and kissed me on the cheek! Well, I tell you, I was so surprised I lost my balance and nearly fell off the porch. Emma giggled, and darned if I couldn't think of another word to say. We stood there like that, her in the doorway and me staring at her with my mouth hangin' open until at last she asked me if I'd come by for some reason, that is, other than to bring her chocolates.

"'Oh, yes,' I said, suddenly remembering. I pulled the tickets from my pocket. 'I got these,' I said, 'and I wondered if you—'

"'Oooh,' she said, cutting me right off. 'I'm sorry, Sam. I'm already going.'

"Well, that knocked the wind out of my sails. 'You are?' I mumbled.

"'Yes,' she said. 'David Michaels asked me. He's taking me in his new

Packard. Have you seen it? It's just the berries!'

"'Yep,' I told her as I turned away. 'I've seen it.'

"Well, I can tell you, I walked all the way home kicking a stone and try-ing to figure out how long it would take me to save up for a car."

I smiled.

"I felt a little guilty when I got home, though, thinkin' how I'd wasted that paycheck, and what that money would've meant to Mac. But then . . . well, you know how easy it is to twist things around in your mind and make them come out the way you want. What did I have to feel guilty about? I asked myself. He got a bad break, that's all. It wasn't my doin'. And after all, my folks were letting him stay on till he was well—giving him room and board for free. That was more than a lot of folks would've done in those times."

"I'm sure that's true," I said.

Sam nodded and stared down into his cold tea. "Didn't really make me feel a whole lot better, though. Mac didn't have much to say to me the whole rest of the summer, but he got on fine with the rest of the fam-ily. Soon as he got so's he could hobble around, he insisted on helpin' out wherever he could. He'd feed the chickens, weed Ma's kitchen garden, clean and oil Pa's tools. Ma and Pa and Kate grew right fond of him, but between me and him there just seemed to be a whole briar patch of prickly feelings.

"My wages made a big difference to my family, and I was proud of that. Pa was able to get the new starter for the tractor, and Ma bought some extra chickens and started selling eggs up to Greenwich Lake along with her beans. Kate even got a new dress to wear to the Grange Summer Swing. She invited Mac even though he couldn't dance, and he seemed pleased to go. I asked Emma, but as usual, some other fella was there ahead of me. You'd think I woulda got the hint by then, but I didn't. I had my eye on a little old Maxwell roadster out behind the fillin' station. Each week I put my half of my pay in a cigar box in my top drawer. By the end of the summer I figured I'd have enough to make an offer on it. All day long while I was choppin' trees and brush under the hot sun I cooled myself with daydreams of me and Emma speedin' along in that little Maxwell with the wind blowing through our hair."

"Sounds like fun," I said.

Sam laughed. "Oh, sure, the daydreamin' was fun, but when I come home it'd be a different story. I'd catch sight of Mac hobblin' around the hen yard with his crutch, or shellin' beans on the back porch with his stiff leg straight out in front of him, or propped up in bed, brooding over them books of his, and all my happy thoughts would drain away quick as runoff after a storm."

"But why did you feel so guilty?" I asked. "I don't think I would have."

"Well," said Sam, "there was somethin' else I've yet to mention. See, I'd met a few of Mac's old friends on the job and found out about his life back in Boston. Seems he did have family back there, but it wasn't any wonder he didn't want to talk about 'em. Turned out his pa was in jail for killing some guy in a barroom brawl, and his ma had taken up with a hobo who'd come to her back door looking for a handout. Seems the new boyfriend was somethin' of a boozer, and whenever he tied one on, he'd get ornery and slap Mac around."

"Oh," I said quietly. "No wonder he didn't want to go back there."

"Mmm," said Sam. "I remember askin' along toward August what he was gonna do when he got the cast off, but he didn't answer.

"'You still heading to Ohio?' I asked.

"'Don't know,' he said. 'It's a long walk.'

"'You could hitch, or catch a freight,' I suggested.

"' Won't do me much good without books.'

"I remember glancing at my top drawer, knowin' I could give Mac his dream back if I wanted. But the thing is, I had a dream of my own by then, and I wasn't about to give it up.

"'Something'll work out,' I told Mac. 'My ma always says, "Where there's a will there's a way."'

"'Yeah,' Mac said bitterly. 'I used to believe in fairy tales, too.'

"His cast come off later that month. He still had a pretty bad gimp, and Doc said he always would. The leg had healed shorter than his other one, and there was no help for it."

"Life sure seemed determined to beat the kid down, huh?" I said.

Sam nodded. "That night at supper he told us he'd be leavin' the next day. He was asleep when I left for work, so I didn't get to say goodbye. My conscience weighed heavy on me all day, though. See, I didn't have a lot, but I knew I had a lot more than Mac. I sure coulda used that Maxwell, but Mac . . . Mac sure coulda used a break. I kept goin' back and forth in my mind like that, but by the end of the day I'd managed to convince myself that Mac wasn't my responsibility. I figured if he was tough enough, he'd still make his dream come true somehow. And if not, well, those were the breaks.

"'Mac gone yet?' I asked Ma when I got home.

"'He left a couple of hours ago,' she said. 'He said to tell you he'd be in touch.'

"I remember thinking that was odd. After all, we'd hardly even spoken while he was there. Why would he be in touch? I put it down to bein' one of those meaningless things folks say when parting, and I went on up to my room.

"I stared at Mac's bed and at the dresser with all his books gone, and I felt kind of empty. I'd liked him, you see, and I'd thrown away our chance to be friends because of the money. I was angry at myself, and I went over to my top drawer and pulled the cigar box out. I flipped it open and looked inside . . . and danged if it wasn't empty."

"No way!" I said. "He took the money?"

"Yep," said Sam. "Shocked me, too. I dropped the box and ran downstairs.

"'Which way did he go?' I asked my mother.

"'Toward town,' she said. 'Why?'

"The bus station, I realized. I ran out of the house and jumped on my bike and pedaled like mad the whole five miles into town. Just as I come over the last rise I saw him dead ahead. The sight of him drew me up short, and I stopped and tried to think what I should do. That's when that messsage come back to me—the one he'd given my mother. I couldn't help wonderin' if that'd been his way of saying he meant to pay me back someday."

"Even so, that still didn't make it right," I said.

"No. No, it didn't," said Sam. "But you know something? As I stood there, watching him limp along, lugging his lumpy satchel of dreams, I figured out somethin'. I figured out that there was a fine line between need and greed, and that line was right there between me and Mac."

"So what'd you do?" I asked.

"I turned around and rode home."

"Without saying a word?"

"Without saying a word."

"Did you ever hear from him again?" I asked.

"Nope," said Sam, "but we left the valley soon after that. The commission said it was time to go. Kate and I moved in with friends in Athol so's we could finish our schoolin' and my folks went on the road doin' migrant work. Once I finished high school, I joined the Civilian Conservation Corps and moved around quite a lot. So I don't know if Mac ever tried to reach me or not. I like to think he did, though."

Sam looked out the window as though he still expected that Mac might come walking up his front steps any day now.

"Whatever happened with Emma?" I asked.

Sam glanced at me, and his cheeks reddened like a schoolboy's. His eyes flicked in the direction of an old photograph that was stuck to the front of his refrigerator, and a gentle radiance lit his face. "Well," he said softly, "I found May, you see. . . ." ❧

I Want You to
Write to Me

Eleanor Roosevelt

The invitation which forms the title of this page comes from my heart, in the hope that we can establish here a clearing house, a discussion room, for the millions of men, women and young people who read the *Companion* every month.

For years I have been receiving letters from all sorts of persons living in every part of our country. Always I have wished that I could reach these correspondents and many more with messages which perhaps might help them, their families, their neighbors and friends to solve the problems which are forever rising in our personal, family and community lives, not only with my ideas but with the ideas of others.

And now I have a department in this magazine which I can use in this way. The editor of the *Woman's Home Companion* has given me this page to do exactly as I will; but you must help me. I want you to tell me about the particular problems which puzzle or sadden you, but also I want you to write me about what has brought joy to your life, and how you are adjusting yourself to the new conditions in this amazing changing world.

I want you to write to me freely. Your confidence will not be betrayed. Your name will not be printed unless you give permission. Do not hesitate to write to me even if your views clash with what you believe to be my views.

We are passing through a time which perhaps presents to us more serious difficulties than the days immediately after the war,[1] but my own

1 **war:** World War I, 1914-1918

experience has been that all times have their own problems. Times of great material prosperity bring their own spiritual problems, for our characters are apt to suffer more in such periods than in times when the narrowed circumstances of life bring out our sturdier qualities; so whatever happens in our lives, we find questions constantly recurring that we would gladly discuss with some friend. Yet it is hard to find just the friend we should like to talk to. Often it is easier to write to someone whom we do not expect ever to see. We can say things which we cannot say to the average individual we meet in our daily lives.

To illustrate the changing nature of our problems it is interesting to remember that less than twenty years ago the outstanding problem of the American homemaker was food conservation, or how to supply proper nourishment for her family with one hand while helping to feed an army with the other![2] Ten years ago the same mothers were facing the problem of postwar extravagance and recklessness; how to control the luxurious tastes of their children, the craving for gayety, pleasure, speed which always follows a great war. Today in millions of homes parents are wrestling with the problem of providing the necessities of life for their children and honest work for the boys and girls who are leaving school.

At almost stated intervals the pendulum swings, and so far the American people have each time solved their problems. And solve them we will again, but not without earnest consultation and reasoning together. Which is exactly where this page enters the national picture.

Let us first consider one or two typical problems. You all know that in May the entire nation celebrated Child Health Week. I was among those who spoke on the basic foundations on which the health of a child is built. A few days after I gave this radio talk I received a letter from a mother who wanted to know how she could supply nourishing food and proper clothing for her three children when her husband was earning exactly fifty-four dollars a month!

Again, a couple who had read something I had said about modern methods in education wrote asking what trades or professions would offer the best opportunities for young people in the next few years.

You will note that both of these earnest letters came from parents.

---

2 **while helping to feed an army with the other:** During World War I, families were encouraged to donate vegetables from their gardens to support the war effort.

This is encouraging, for there never was a time when the sympathy and tolerance of older people were more needed to help the younger people adjust themselves to a very difficult world.

In the hands of the young people lies the future of this country, perhaps the future of the world and our civilization. They need what help they can get from the older generation and yet it must be sympathetically given with a knowledge that in the last analysis the young people themselves must make their own decisions.

You will be reading this page in midsummer when discussion of the summer vacation is paramount in many American homes. I am an enthusiastic believer in vacations. They are, in my opinion, an investment paying high dividends in mental and physical health.

So this month I am going to ask you a question. We all know that we have less money to spend on recreation than we have had for a great many years. How can we make that money cover the needs of a real holiday? I should like to have those of you who have taken holidays inexpensively to tell me what you have done.

Perhaps you will be interested in a holiday I myself enjoyed many years ago.

We took four young boys to whom we wanted to show some points of historical interest, at the same time giving them a thoroughly healthful trip. We decided to take our car and strap on the side of it one big tent and one pup tent. The four boys slept in sleeping bags with their heads under the pup tent if it rained. We ran about one hundred and fifty miles a day. We would buy our supplies in some village through which we passed in the late afternoon. Then we would make camp near some river or brook, usually finding a hospitable farmer who would supply us with milk, butter and eggs.

We had to cook our supper and make our camp before it was dark after which we would have a swim and sit around, talk or read and go to bed in

Eleanor Roosevelt during a radio broadcast, 1934

the twilight. We were up again at dawn and during the day we would stop and see whatever historical things might be of interest on the way. Our route ran north through New York State so that we saw Ausable Chasm, the shores of Lake Champlain. We stopped a day in Montreal and two days in Quebec; then we drove down through the White Mountains where we camped two days in order to climb some of them on burros, to the great joy of the children; then east through the beautiful central part of Maine with its lakes and woods, down to the sea to Castine, and home by the road along the shore.

Our actual camping trip lasted ten days and cost us only the wear and tear on the car, the gasoline and oil, and our simple food, with a very little extra for admissions, for donkeys to climb the mountains and the cog railway up Mt. Washington, but these of course could have been eliminated. This was one of the least expensive holidays I have ever taken and it could easily be duplicated with profit and health for all concerned.

A less elaborate trip may prove quite as satisfying. A week or two in a good camp has its advantages if swimming, fishing, and hiking are available, and even weekend picnicking will break the monotony of summer in city or small town.

If you have taken such a trip with family or friends, won't you tell me about your experiences, giving sufficient detail to serve those who wish to duplicate your vacation. Your plan may be just the one I should be glad to pass on to other *Companion* readers.

Please do not imagine that I am planning to give you advice that will eventually solve all your problems. We all know that no human being is infallible, and on this page I am not setting myself up as an oracle.[3] But it may be that in the varied life I have had there have been certain experiences which other people will find useful, and it may be that out of the letters which come to me I shall learn of experiences which will prove helpful to others.

And so I close my first page to you and for you, as I opened it, with a cordial invitation—I want you to write to me. ∾

---

3 **oracle:** a person giving wise decisions or opinions

LETTERS TO THE ROOSEVELTS

Chicago Ill 4/3—35
Mrs. F. D. Roosevelt
Washington D.C.

Dear Mrs. Roosevelt: —

Please pardon the liberty I am taking in writing you this note. Like thousands of others have lost and used up what we have saved, have been forced to go on relief. Have been compelled to store the small amt of things we had, and live in one room which is detrimental to our health. and unless we can raise our storage chg. Amt $28 by 4/10 the things may be sold for storage while not so valuable to any one else there are things that Cannot be replaced. I would like to borrow the amt $28 so I can pay the chg. and get a More healthful place to live. We are American born citizens and have always been self-supporting. It is very humiliating for me to have to write you Asking you again to pardon the privilege I am taking. I am hoping I may hear from you without publicity by ret. post.

Very Respectfully
Mrs. [Initials omitted because of writer's request]

Troy, N.Y.
Jan. 2, 1935.

Dear Mrs. Roosevelt,

About a month ago I wrote you asking if you would buy some baby clothes for me with the understanding that I was to repay you as soon as my husband got enough work. Several weeks later I received a reply to apply to a Welfare Association so I might receive the aid I needed. Do you remember?

Please Mrs. Roosevelt, I do not want charity, only a chance from someone who will trust me until we can get enough money to repay the amount spent for the things I need. As a proof that I really am sincere, I am sending you two of my dearest possessions to keep as security, a ring my husband gave me before we were married, and a ring my mother used to wear. Perhaps the actual value of them is not high, but they are worth a lot to me. If you will consider buying the baby clothes, please keep them (rings) until I send you the money you spent. It is very hard to face bearing a baby we cannot afford to have, and the fact that it is due to arrive soon, and still there is no money for the hospital or clothing, does not make it any easier. I Have decided to stay home, keeping my 7 year old daughter from school to help with the smaller children when my husband has work.

The oldest little girl is sick now, and has never been strong, so I would not depend on her. The 7 year old one is a good willing little worker and somehow we must manage—but without charity.

If you still feel you cannot trust me, it is allright and I can only say I donot blame you, but if you decide my word is worth anything with so small a security, here is a list of what I will need—but I will need it very soon.

2 shirts, silk and wool. size 2
3 pr. stockings, silk and wool, 4 1/2 or 4
3 straight flannel bands
2 slips—outing flannel
2 muslim dresses
1 sweater
1 wool bonnet
2 pr. wool booties
2 doz. diapers 30 x 30—or 27 x 27
1 large blanket (baby) about 15" or 50"
3 outing flannel nightgaowns

If you will get these for me I would rather no one knew about it. I promise to repay the cost of the layette as soon as possible. We will all be very grateful to you, and I will be more than happy.

Sincerely yours,
Mrs. H. E. C.

May 1936
Hattiesburg Miss

Mr Presedent Sir We are starving in Hattiesburg we poor White's + Negros too i wish you could See the poor hungry an naket half clad's at the relief office an is turned away With tears in their eys Mississippi is made her own laws an dont treat her destuted as her Pres. has laid the plans for us to live if <u>the</u> leg-islators would do as our good Pres. has Said What few days we have here we could be happy in our last old days both old white + Colard

Cencerely looking for our old age pension's an will thank you they has made us Sighn for $ 3 00 a Month Cant live at that

[Anonymous]

[February, 1936]
Mr. and Mrs. Roosevelt.
Wash. D. C.

Dear Mr. President:

I'm a boy of 12 years. I want to tell you about my family. My father hasn't worked for 5 months. He went plenty times to relief, he filled out application. They won't give us anything. I don't know why. Please you do something. We haven't paid 4 months rent, Everyday the landlord rings the door bell, we don't open the door for him. We are afraid that will be put out, been put out before, and don't want to happen again. We haven't paid the gas bill, and the electric bill, haven't paid grocery bill for 3 months. My brother goes to Lane Tech. High. School. he's eighteen years old, hasn't gone to school for 2 weeks because he got no carfare. I have a sister she's twenty years, she can't find work. My father he staying home. All the time he's crying because he can't find work. I told him why are you crying daddy, and daddy said why shouldn't I cry when there is nothing in the house. I feel sorry for him. That night I couldn't sleep. The next morning I wrote this letter to you. in my room. Were American citizens and were born in Chicago, Ill. and I don't know why they don't help us Please answer right away because we need it. will starve Thank you.

God bless you.
[Anonymous]
Chicago, Ill.

VOICES OF DISCONTENT

GAIL B. STEWART

Franklin Roosevelt might have been hailed as a superman in 1932 as he took office, but by the end of his first year as president, reality had set in. The New Deal programs had put millions back to work, but there were still millions more without work. There had been months of improvement with definite signs of recovery, but there had also been months in which the economy slipped downward.

And because recovery had not been automatic, Roosevelt began to be the focus of criticism by various groups of Americans.

Complaints from the Rich

Some of Roosevelt's most harsh criticism came from the powerful people—the owners of businesses and captains of industry, bankers, investors, and other wealthy people. These people, whose banks, businesses, and investments were being threatened, were very relieved when Roosevelt took office. Yet, as historians have noted wryly, as soon as they were saved, the nation's rich began to get nervous. As Roosevelt and his Brain Trust put more and more New Deal programs into practice, the wealthy discovered that Roosevelt's goal was not to get things back to the way they were before the stock market crash of 1929, but rather to change and reform the nation's economy.

When Roosevelt pushed new taxes on the rich through Congress for the purpose of funding more New Deal legislation, that was the last straw. His political enemies branded him a socialist, saying if Roosevelt had his way, the federal government would be running everything, and that private enterprise would be a thing of the past. Rumors abounded that Roosevelt and his Brain Trust wanted to "Russianize"[1] America, and make the nation a dictatorship.

Senator Thomas Schall of Minnesota called the president "Frankenstein Roosevelt" and the NRA blue eagle[2] "that Soviet duck." And Henry Ford, one of the richest, most influential men in America, made no secret of the fact that he refused to support the NRA codes. "Hell, that Roosevelt buzzard!" he scoffed. "I wouldn't put it on the car."

The growing fury among the rich was much publicized for the simple reason that the largest newspapers were run by wealthy families. William Randolph Hearst, one of the most successful newspaper giants in the United States, wrote scathing editorials against Roosevelt and the NRA. Hearst and other newspaper publishers were especially angry about the NRA's banning of child labor, for in those days newspapers depended for their circulation on the young newsboys who worked for ridiculously low wages.

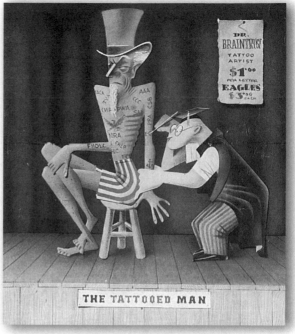

Newspaper cartoonists often criticized Roosevelt's "Alphabet Soup" of government programs.

Criticism from the Left

Interestingly, as big business was growing more vocal about what they called Roosevelt's swing toward socialism, prominent American socialists were angry with the president for being too nice to big business. On a political continuum, with the left being socialism, socialists thought Roosevelt was too far right. Norman Thomas, a socialist who rejected the New Deal because it was too capitalistic, insisted that the president "did

1 **Russianize:** to make Russian; the Russian revolution of 1917 imposed a Communist economy where the state managed all production and divided goods and services among all its citizens. Josef Stalin, a strict Communist, was Russia's dictator in 1932.

2 **NRA blue eagle:** A blue eagle was the symbol used by Roosevelt's National Recovery Administration

not carry out the Socialist platform unless he carried it out on a stretcher."

Others agreed with Thomas, and the mid-1930s saw several movements from the political left which, at least temporarily, seemed to offer depression-weary Americans a glimmer of hope. One of these was a program called End Poverty in California (EPIC), founded by Upton Sinclair.

He devised a plan that he claimed would totally eliminate poverty within four years. The plan was socialistic, in that it called for government ownership of all factories and businesses. Large community farms would replace the small family farms in the United States. And because such a large segment of California's population was elderly, Sinclair's plan also called for a monthly pension of $60 to all people over 60.

Townsend Clubs

Dr. Francis Townsend was another California Roosevelt critic whose special cause was the elderly. He had become active in this cause after an incident that happened in 1933, shortly after Roosevelt took office.

Townsend's plan was that the government pay $200 per month to every American over age 60, provided that each recipient agreed to spend the money within 30 days. Townsend believed that his plan would end the depression, for there would be more money in circulation, in the hands of wise older Americans who would not spend money foolishly.

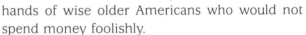

Father Charles Coughlin

The Radio Priest

One of the most popular of the anti-Roosevelt political extreme was a Catholic priest, Father Charles Edward Coughlin. Father Coughlin had a weekly radio show called "The Golden Hour of the Little Flower," which he broadcast from a suburb of Detroit, Michigan.

Politically, Coughlin began as a Roosevelt supporter in the election of 1932. He called then-president Hoover "the banker's friend, the Holy Ghost of the rich, the protective angel of Wall Street." He liked Roosevelt, and during the Hundred Days stated frequently in his broadcasts that "the New Deal is Christ's deal."

But he lost patience with Roosevelt and his Brain Trust, believing that the Democratic party was not moving fast enough to solve the problems of poverty. Like Sinclair, Coughlin embraced socialism, claiming that the nation would be better off if the government ran the industries.

Father Coughlin told his listeners that bankers were "devils" and that their overwhelming lust for profits was the cause of the unemployed and widespread poverty in the United States. As for Coughlin himself, he claimed that his task was to remind the government of its moral obligation to the people. "I glory in the fact that I am a simple Catholic priest," Coughlin remarked, "endeavoring to inject Christianity into the fabric of an economic system woven upon the loom of the greedy."

An anti-Semitic,[3] Coughlin believed that Roosevelt's New Deal had been infested with the wealthy Jewish bankers, and that what had begun as good programs were now corrupt. He called Roosevelt's administration "government of the bankers, by the bankers, and for the bankers."

Coughlin's ideas became more and more radical in the 1930s. He lost most of his popularity as he began to preach about the need for a dictatorship in America, especially when he embraced the political ideals of Adolf Hitler and Benito Mussolini.

"Every Man a King"

But it was Senator Huey Long from Louisiana who was the most famous critic of Roosevelt. Long was known to his millions of supporters as "the Kingfish" because of his philosophy of "Every man a king, every girl a queen" that made him so popular in his home state.

Long thought it was disgraceful that there could be multimillionaires in the United States when millions were living below the poverty level. He proposed that the enormous wealth in the United States be shared so that everyone could have enough. He called his program Share Our Wealth.

Under Long's plan, inheritances would be limited to $5 million, and no personal fortune could exceed $8 million. The government's job would be to take control of any excess money and redistribute it among needy families. The goal was to provide every family in America with a free car, a home, a radio, and an annual income of $2,000. In addition, Share Our Wealth would guarantee every young man and woman a free college education.

None of this occurred however, because in September 1935 a Louisiana physician who had a longtime grievance against Long assassinated him. ∾

Senator Huey Long

3 **anti-Semitic:** one who discriminates against Jews

Responding to Cluster Two

What Was the New Deal?

Thinking Skill SUMMARIZING

1. The nonfiction piece "Built to Last," and the fiction piece, "Brother, Can You Spare a Dream" both deal with the Civilian Conservation Corps. In which selection did you learn more about how it felt to be a part of the Corps? Explain your answer.

2. **Compare and contrast** Eleanor Roosevelt's letter to the readers of *Woman's Home Companion* in "I Want You to Write to Me" to the letters she received in "Letters to the Roosevelts." What differences can you infer between the readers of the *Woman's Home Companion* and the people who wrote to the Roosevelts?

3. Do you think Arvel Pearson from "King of the Hoboes" would have given up riding the rails to participate in a program such as the Civilian Conservation Corps?

4. What does the title "Brother, Can You Spare a Dream?" mean?

5. Not everyone was satisfied with Franklin D. Roosevelt's plans. **Summarize** the proposed alternatives as presented in "Voices of Discontent."

Writing Activity: An Encyclopedia Entry

Imagine you are writing entries for an encyclopedia. **Summarize** Franklin D. Roosevelt's New Deal using no more than 150 words. Check an encyclopedia for an appropriate writing style.

An Encyclopedia Entry

• covers the topic thoroughly but includes only the most important points

• uses precise unbiased language

• uses an encyclopedia entry format

CLUSTER THREE

How Tough Were the Times?

Thinking Skill   ANALIZING

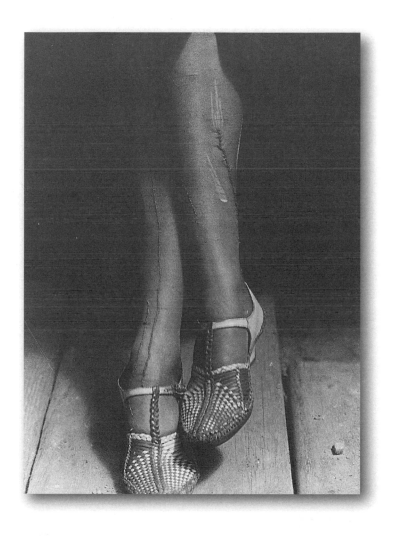

DIGGING IN

ROBERT J. HASTINGS

The closing of Old West Side Mine meant the end of anything resembling a steady job for the next eight years. From 1930 on, it was a day's work here and a day's work there, a coal order from the welfare office, a relief check, a few days on WPA,[1] a garden in the back yard, and a few chickens and eggs.

We weathered the storm because of Dad's willingness to take any job and Mom's ability to stretch every available dollar. It was not so much a matter of finding a job as of filling in with odd jobs wherever and whenever you could, and most of the "jobs" were those you made for yourself.

My diary shows that Dad sold iron cords door to door, "worked a day in the hay," bought a horse to break gardens, rented an extra lot for a garden on the shares, picked peaches, raised sweet potato slips, traded an occasional dozen of eggs at the grocery, hung wallpaper, "painted Don Albright's house for $5," picked up a day or two's work at the strip mines, guarded the fence at the county fairgrounds, cut hair for boys in the neighborhood, sold coal orders, and when he had to and could, worked intermittently on WPA.

With no dependable income, we cut back on everything possible. We stopped the evening paper, turned off the city water and cleaned out our well, sold our four-door Model T touring car with the snap-on side curtains and isinglass,[2] stopped ice and milk delivery, and disconnected our gas range for all but the three hot summer months. There was no telephone to disconnect, as we didn't have one to start with!

1 **WPA:** Works Progress Administration
2 **isinglass:** another name for mica, a mineral that flakes into transparent sheets which can be used as a substitute for glass

We did keep up regular payments on two Metropolitan Life Insurance policies. Page after page of old receipt books show entries of 10¢ per week on one policy and 69¢ a month on another. As long as we could, we made house payments to the Marion Building and Loan, but a day came when we had to let those go, too.

Fortunately, we were able to save our house from foreclosure. When so many borrowers defaulted, the Marion Building and Loan went bankrupt. Creditors were allowed to pay just about any amount to satisfy the receivers. But that was the catch—who had "just about any amount" to pay? A house behind ours sold for $25. Many good houses in Marion sold for $5 to $100 and were torn down and moved to nearby towns. We settled with the loan company for $125, or ten cents on the dollar for our $1250 mortgage. I'll never forget the day Dad cleared it all up, making two or three trips to town to bring papers home for Mom to sign. He was able to borrow the $125 from his aunt, Dialtha James, who as the widow of a Spanish-American War veteran had a small pension.

Looking back, I find it amazing what we did without. A partial list would include toothpaste (we used soda), toilet paper (we used the catalog), newspaper or magazine subscriptions, soft drinks, potato chips and snacks, bakery goods except bread and an occasional dozen of doughnuts, paper clips, rubber bands, and restaurant meals. We had no water bill, sewer bill, telephone bill, no car expenses—gasoline, tires, batteries, licenses, insurance, repairs—no laundry service, no dry cleaning (we pressed woolens with a hot iron and a wet cloth), no bank service charge (no bank account), no sales or income tax. We sent no greeting cards except maybe half a dozen at Christmas.

There were no convenience or frozen foods, vitamin tablets, bandaids, kleenex, paper towels. Garbage pickup, TV and TV repairs, long-distance calls, health insurance, Scotch-tape—these necessities of today were unknown to us then.

Typical of the simple economies that Mom practiced was keeping the electric bill to $1 a month and the gas bill to $1 a month in June, July, and August. I know, because I rode my bicycle to town to pay these bills.

Since our only appliance was an electric iron, the chief use of electricity was for lighting. With only a single bulb suspended by a cord from the ceiling of each room, there weren't many lights to burn, even if they were all turned on at the same time. But that's the point—they weren't. On winter evenings Mom would turn on the kitchen light while she cooked supper. If I had lessons I brought them to the kitchen table or sprawled on the floor between the kitchen and dining room.

After supper we "turned off the light in the kitchen" and moved to the dining-sitting room, where another light was switched on. If we wanted to read on winter afternoons, we sat as near a window as possible, with the curtains pinned back, to save the lights until it was nearly dark. In the summer we often made our way to bed in the dark, not so much to save a penny or two as to "keep the house cool" and not attract the bugs.

When ironing, Mom saved flat pieces such as towels and handkerchiefs to the last, to be pressed while the iron was cooling and the electricity was off. To save gas in the summer, she planned her meals to make maximum use of the oven, so if she was roasting meat, she would also be baking cookies. Utensils were often stacked two deep on the range so that a boiling pot of beans would help to cook the potatoes.

Dad had some old-fashioned shoe lasts,[3] and he would buy stick-'em-on soles at the dime store to patch our shoes in winter. With simple barber tools he cut my hair and that of other kids in the neighborhood, for maybe ten cents a head. In cold, wet weather when he worked outdoors on WPA he often cut strips of cardboard to stuff in the soles of his shoes and keep his feet warm.

We took care of what we had. Every cotton cloth was used over as a dish cloth, wash cloth, dust cloth, shoe-shining cloth, window-washing cloth, to scrub and wax floors, make bandages, make quilt pieces, make kite tails, or to tie boxes and papers together. The cotton bags from flour, salt, or cracked chicken feed were washed, bleached, and cut into dish cloths and towels. Some neighbors made curtains or even dresses from feed sacks. Every paper bag was saved for lunches or cut and used for wrapping paper. String was wound into balls for later use.

---

3 **shoe last:** a foot-shaped form over which a shoe is placed for repair.

Each August Mom would find someone who was a year ahead of me in school, and buy his used books. One exception was a spelling book used in all eight grades. Since it was to be used for eight years, we decided it would be a wise investment to buy a new one when I started first grade. In the seventh grade, I dropped that speller in the snow. I thought Mom was unfair when she sent me all the way back to school, retracing my steps to look for the book. Fortunately, I found it about two-thirds of the way back.

Sometimes, over a weekend, Mom would count out enough slices of bread to make my lunches for the following week. They would be set aside and used for nothing else. She did the same for Dad's lunch if he happened to be working, as we bought groceries only once a week. If she baked an angel food cake, she saved back enough for lunches each day of the week. She usually wrapped my lunch in newspaper and tied it with a string.

Before the Depression, we hung a four-cornered black-and-white card-board sign in the front window each morning. The figures in the corners told the iceman how many pounds to bring—25, 50, 75, or 100. But ice was one of the casualties of the Depression, although we managed a small piece two or three times a week for iced tea. About eleven in the morning I would pull a little wagon, filled with a gunny sack and assorted old quilts and tarpaulins, down to the neighborhood ice house to buy "a nickel's worth of ice," which was half of a 25-pound chunk. By wrapping it carefully and storing it in a cool, damp spot under the house, we could stretch that piece of ice for two or three days. In rainy, cool weather, maybe four days! It was our glistening prize, and any left over from tea was emptied back into a pitcher of ice water, or used for lemonade that afternoon. So as not to waste any, we chipped only what was needed, with much of the same care used by a diamond cutter.

Whatever was free was our recreation. This may have included playing records on our wind-up victrola or listening to the Atwater-Kent radio. You might watch a parachute jump at the airport or a free ball game at the city park, with perhaps a free band concert afterwards and the side attraction of a watermelon-eating contest (with your hands tied behind you). The band concerts survived only the first two years of the Depression.

Or you might go out to the airport hangar to watch the dance marathon, cringe at the risks taken by the Dodge-'Em cars at the fairgrounds on Labor Day, or attend a medicine show where the hawker peddled a single elixir said to cure everything from arthritis to zymosis.[4] There were family dinners and picnics, and occasionally four or five families would pile into the back of Ted Boles' coal truck for an overnight camping-fishing trip to the Ohio River at Shawneetown or Metropolis.

We liked music, and one of my earliest memories is of Dad singing to me:

marathon dancers

Two arms that hold me tight,
Two lips that kiss goodnight;
To me he'll always be,
That little boy of mine.

No one can ever know,
Just what his coming has meant;
He's something heaven has sent,
That little boy of mine.

4 **zymosis:** an infectious disease caused by a fungus

One spring morning he came in and sat on the edge of my bed. I had been sick a few days, but now the sun was shining and he was encouraging me to get up and play. Outside the birds were singing.

"Do you know what the birds are singing?" he asked me.

"No."

"They're singing, 'Bobby get up, Bobby get up . . .' "

When I was small, Dad taught me a ballad that I would sometimes perform for visiting relatives, standing on the footstool as I sang:

Oh hand me down my walking cane,
Oh hand me down my walking cane,
Oh hand me down my walking cane,
For I'm gonna leave on that midnight train,
For all my sins are taken away, taken away.

Now if I die in Tennessee,
Now if I die in Tennessee,
Now if I die in Tennessee,
Ship me back by C.O.D.,
For all my sins are taken away, taken away.

The lament continued with several verses: "Oh I got drunk, and I got in jail . . . had no one to go my bail . . . the beans was tough, and the meat was fat . . . come on Momma, and go my bail, get me out of this buggy jail . . . for all my sins are taken away, taken away."

At one point in the Depression, the cupboard was literally bare of money. We weren't hungry, but we were penniless. Then Dad went back in the pantry and came out with a jar in which he had saved a few nickels and dimes for such an emergency.

Later, Mom said to me, "I've learned that whatever happens, your Daddy always has a little dab of money put back somewhere . . ." ❧

THE LESSON

HARRY MARK PETRAKIS

When I was in my green-boned youth, a little less than twelve, we lived in a neighborhood that was a village within the city. Prohibition had just been repealed, the banks had closed, and the country was in the grip of the hungry years.

Looking back from our vantage point today, everything seemed astonishingly cheap. A box of cornflakes cost eight cents, a quart of milk a dime, a dental filling a dollar. Yet inexpensive as everything might have been made little difference because money to buy anything was so scarce.

My father was a Greek Orthodox priest with his parish in a south side neighborhood. In addition to my mother, there were six children in our family, three boys and three girls. Four siblings were older than I was and a sister was younger. The four oldest worked part-time jobs and contributed to expenses. My sister and I were spared outside employment because of our ages but helped my mother in her housework and by running errands.

For a period of several years, we moved every year. I suspect those moves came because new tenants were allowed the first two month's free rent. Yet each of the apartments we occupied in the three story buildings had the same bleak, cramped interiors, small bedrooms and still smaller bathrooms, like cubicles in the labyrinth of Daedalus.[1]

The warmest and most convivial room in the apartment was always the kitchen. There my mother daily replicated the miracle of the loaves

---

1 **labyrinth of Daedalus:** a legendary maze in Crete built by the artist Daedalus. Here it means a building with confusing passageways.

and fishes.[2] The Greek rice dish, pilaf, was one of her staples and she prepared it several times a week in great pots. Yet with culinary cunning she dismembered one scrawny chicken into each pot of pilaf. In her wisdom she understood a morsel of poultry suggested a more wholesome meal. My sister and I, being the youngest, were often left with the less palatable parts of the fowl. But I did not know they were undesirable then and I confess those meals have left me with a propensity for the chicken's tail and neck.

The cloistered[3] neighborhood in which we lived was populated by several ethnic and religious groups. There were Greek Orthodox and Italian Catholics, and Russian and Polish Jews. We lived and played together amicably because poverty compelled us into democracy. How could I harbor any prejudice against a Catholic or Jewish boy whose pants were ragged as mine?

Little was known of family planning then, so large families were the norm. To clothe the mob of children was an imposing challenge. The only clothing store in our neighborhood was owned by a wily shopkeeper who handled only two sizes. "A perfect fit!" or "He'll grow into it!"

In his emporium,[4] clothing was not displayed on racks but piled in great mounds on several large tables. The piles might include a few new items but most of the clothing was used. To see a half dozen mothers foraging through piles to find garments suitable for their offspring could only be compared to an army seeking plunder.

But there was very little cash to pay for store-bought clothing whether used or new. So an energetic activity of the mothers was the ancient trade of barter.

In this exchange of clothing, my mother was a skillful contestant. She had an intuitive sense about which boys and girls in our block were outgrowing their dresses and jackets the quickest and which of these garments could be accommodated to the needs of our family.

It was true that for a good part of the year we wore as little clothing as possible. The boy's attire was a simple pair of pants, t-shirt, socks and battered sneakers. The girls wore plain dresses or shorts. However, as fall began to chill our days, we needed more durable apparel. So the first traces of colder weather compelled a frenzy of haggling. Mothers would

---

2 **miracle of the loaves and fishes:** In the Bible, Jesus Christ transforms five loaves of bread and two fish into enough food to feed thousands of people.

3 **cloistered:** sheltered from the outside world

4 **emporium:** store

visit one another after dinner carrying an armful of clothing. A girl's dress for a boy's shirt. A boy's blazer for a girl's jacket.

In the same way that we tended to be tolerant of one another's ethnicity and religion, we were forbearing of the shabby and mismatched clothing that graced our lithe, young bodies. Clothing was something we wore to keep us decent. From time to time some aberration drew our derision but those taunts passed quickly. That is until the appearance of the green and yellow coat.

So many years have passed since then that I wonder if I am making that coat more appalling than it really was. Lacking the vocabulary at the time to properly describe the garment, in recalling it now, the words hideous and ghastly come to mind.

The coat first appeared on a late November afternoon worn by my next-door neighbor, Seymour. He was about a year older than I was, ten pounds heavier, with a doleful demeanor. Or perhaps I remember it as doleful because the coat belonged to him.

Seymour emerged from the hallway of his building. A half dozen of us at play in the street fell silent, staring at the approaching apparition. The colors were what struck us first. A sickly green and a pallid yellow. But the colors also seemed to leak into one another so the yellow had traces of green and the green traces of yellow. In the same way, the material was indefinable, suggesting mostly a kind of frayed wool or threadbare fleece. There was also a ragged belt that Seymour wore as if it were a noose.

Seymour witnessed our collective shock and hesitated, as if pondering whether to flee back inside. By then it was too late. Our relentless taunting and mocking had begun.

All through that cold and dismal winter, Seymour wore that coat that was so ugly it offended even our primitive aesthetic senses. But since the coat was also an inanimate object, all our scorn and ridicule was hurled upon the wearer. He would have gladly thrown it away and borne the elements stoically but his parents warned him somberly that he might fall ill from exposure and die. In the end Seymour endured that winter more wretched than poor Hester Prynne[5] in the Nathaniel Hawthorne novel we studied in school. Her letter was only scarlet while Seymour's coat was yellow and green.

Finally, the worst of winter passed. Then, on a still cold day in early March, a coatless Seymour emerged from his apartment, so

5 **Hester Prynne:** a character in *The Scarlet Letter* who is condemned to wear a scarlet *A* on her clothing as punishment for adultery

buoyant and unburdened he might have been naked. Although we had some cold days later in March and in early April, Seymour never wore that coat again.

April cavorted into May and May frolicked into June. The sun grew stronger and we stripped off layers of clothing until we played, almost naked, our arms, legs and faces growing tanned from the sun.

Yet in that blustery, subzero region known as the Midwest, the sun's reign is transitory. Before we knew it, summer had passed.

As autumn arrived, we prepared for school. The mothers returned like itinerant peddlers to haggling and bartering over clothing.

On a Saturday evening my mother returned from one of the trading sessions. My sisters met her with shrieks at our front door, anxious to see the wardrobe she had assembled for them. I had not given serious attention to what clothing I needed. My mother's vigilant eye took care of that and I trusted in her judgment. That is, until I saw amidst the dresses she had brought for my sisters, the monstrous green and yellow coat she had traded to replace my own worn and outgrown coat.

I pleaded for mercy. At the same time I could not confess to her how we had all tormented poor Seymour. She was a religious lady and might have felt my inheriting the coat was evidence of divine justice. In response to my entreaties, she was sympathetic but also adamant. The coat was all I would have to wear to protect me from the implacable cold of the coming winter.

I had never faced the onslaught of any winter with greater dread than I did that year. I avoided wearing the cursed coat as long as I could. When the weather did finally turn cold I took a circuitous back-alley route to school. A half-block away I removed the coat, bunched it up, and stuffed it into a shopping bag.

In that way I managed to avoid exposure for several weeks. But on a frigid Saturday afternoon in early November my mother sent me to the grocery for eggs and bread. Despite my insistence that I'd run both ways, she made me wear the coat.

I purchased the items from the grocery, ignoring the look of pity on the grocer's face. As I emerged from the store I came face to face with a cluster of my friends about to enter the store. Seymour was with them.

I was close enough to witness the shock and disbelief on their faces. That turned quickly to sadistic glee. As their raucous taunts began, Seymour stepped forward quickly and aligned himself beside me. Staring defiantly at the jeering mob, he put his arm protectively and reassuringly around my shoulders. That gesture of defense and support from someone who had suffered our taunts through an entire winter startled the others. They could not comprehend such magnanimity of spirit and it awed and silenced them. In an awkward hush, they turned and shuffled away. And in that glowing moment, Seymour and I bonded like comrades. I understood that because of his greatness of soul, I had been spared.

Now, a lifetime later, as I recount this story, I am intemperately moved once again. What befell me then in my twelfth year of life was a lesson in tolerance and forgiveness so searing and unforgettable, it rivaled one of those Greek dramas in which my ancestors portrayed heroes and gods. ∾

Black Sunday

From *The Dirty Thirties*

Thelma Bemount Campbell

I remember that Black Sunday, April 14, 1935.

I was celebrating my birthday with a group of young people and parents who had come home with us from church. I was spending the weekend with my parents at home five miles southeast of May, Oklahoma.

After dinner two carloads of us drove in to town to attend graduation services at the high school. The wind had gone down and it became very still—stifling, hot and sultry. In those days, before air conditioning, all the windows were open, but no air circulated. The speaker didn't arrive on time and everyone was restless and milling around outside watching the sky. There was an anticipation of disaster in the air and everyone was nervous. Some even went home.

The speaker was late, having been lost on unmarked highways. The ceremony was over about four o'clock and it was still hot and threatening. No one had been able to keep his mind on the speaker. We were hoping for rain but afraid at the same time that we would get a devastating hailstorm. One extreme usually followed another when it had been so very dry.

When I arrived home I stopped the car by the back door. My folks had just arrived from a funeral. The wind had turned to the north and we could see it rolling toward us at a terrific speed, like a prairie fire—except there was no fire. Then it became still and black; it was rolling and boiling and the air was full of static electricity. And, since we lived on a high hill, we could see it coming three miles away.

My father was changing clothes to do chores before the storm reached us. I remember telling Dad it was coming fast and asked if I should put the car away. He said he would do it as soon as he could get his shoes on.

I looked again and said, "You don't have time. It's here right now!" And it was upon us.

The wind was so strong that we heard later it had broken the wind gauges. Birds had flown in front of it, rabbits scurried to get out of its path. We could hear their frightened calls. It was terrifying. When it hit, everything became very still and we were enveloped in this terrible blackness. We couldn't see our hand in front of our face. Some people thought they had been struck blind. Of course we were all frightened but there was nothing we could do. My girl friend and I were watching from the north window; we grabbed each other and put our heads down. I felt my time had come and expected to be blown away. It was an eerie feeling. It was so pitch dark that I couldn't even see the outline of my grandmother who was sitting by an east window.

I wanted to light a lamp but my father said, "No, better not even strike a match."

I have no idea how long the blackness lasted, but it seemed an eternity. Some say about an hour before the worst was over. As the eye passed over us the wind remained in the north behind it. It was morning before it finally cleared. Everything was covered with dirt and dust.

We decided we were all right and began to check with our neighbors. The ones that were caught in their cars were quite shook up, saying the car lights couldn't penetrate that darkness. They had to stop and sit it out beside the road.

I doubt that anyone living will ever forget that black Sunday. I'm in my eighties and I can still see that black cloud rolling in.

That is just one part of what I remember about the dirty thirties, following the Great Depression with the stock market crash of 1929. Going back in time, I was a young school teacher at the time of the crash and getting $100 a month and sending myself to summer school to keep my two-year certificate renewed and working toward a lifetime certificate. I was teaching at Kokomo, a rural school near Beaver, Oklahoma.

In the fall of 1929 I had obtained the first and second grade at my home town of May with wages of $90 a month. Although I was only five miles from home, we were required to board in the district and to take part in community affairs. Our board and room took one third of our wages.

Teachers were a dime a dozen at that time and rules were very rigid. If you wanted to keep your job you had to be an example for children to follow. No smoking, drinking, dancing or card playing—and church attendance was a must. No going with high school students either. These rules were written in your contract.

Children were taught to respect their parents and teachers. There were no discipline problems.

By the school year of 1930–1931 the drought and depression were beginning to be felt, so teachers' wages were cut to $85; then by 1932–1933 we were hired for $75 and before spring we were cut to $60—and there wasn't even money to pay that amount. That was before state aid. We were given warrants in five and ten dollar units. We traded them for our needs if we could find someone willing to do so. They weren't redeemed for five years.

By that time President Roosevelt had started the WPA[1] and all the men were trying to get jobs on the roads; those with good teams of horses had the best chances. They were willing to do anything to feed their families. The drought was getting very bad by 1933.

I had taught at May for four years and needed a change. I tried to get

---

1 **WPA:** Works Progress Administration

into a nursing school, a life-long dream, but it was full for the year so I moved to the Luther Hill community and taught the primary grades there. I boarded with a young couple named Turner and Margaret Barret. They lived a mile north of the school house and I walked to and from school.

The wind blew in hurricane force many days. One day it blew from the south and the next from the north. It was so strong some days I could hardly stand up. The dust blew and blew. By the time I reached school I needed a bath. My eyes were full and my teeth gritty. It blew sand in the fence rows and many were completely buried. Wherever there was a thistle or a piece of machinery, it was soon covered. I remember we had to scoop the sand and dust out of our attic at home. It got so full it was causing the plaster to fall. Nothing was tight enough to keep it out. There was no moisture that winter that I can recall now.

The Barrets' house was old with windows and doors that didn't fit very tightly; after the frost that year, there wasn't much to stop the wind. The sand and dust blew in until there was sand in the water bucket, a coating of dust on the water. There was no such thing as running water, indoor plumbing or electricity. So before each meal someone had to get fresh water from the well.

We stuffed rags in the windows to help keep out the dirt. Some times gunny sacks were opened and either dipped in old tractor oil or wet with water, and tacked over the windows to keep out as much dirt as possible.

The beds and furniture were covered with sheets and we had to shake the sheets before we could go to bed on bad days. Some times it was necessary to wet a washcloth and lay it over our nose to breathe.

As spring came it got worse. We cooked and had to wait to clean the table until the last minute. Then we hurriedly set it and ate before the food got gritty. I sincerely hope we never see another drought like that one. It was as if we had moved to the desert. ∽

DROUTH STRICKEN AREA
Alexandre Hogue, 1934

DEBTS

KAREN HESSE

Daddy is thinking
of taking a loan from Mr. Roosevelt and his men,
to get some new wheat planted
where the winter crop has spindled out and died.
Mr. Roosevelt promises
Daddy won't have to pay a dime
till the crop comes in.

Daddy says,
"I can turn the fields over,
start again.
It's sure to rain soon.
Wheat's sure to grow."

Ma says, "What if it doesn't?"

Daddy takes off his hat,
roughs up his hair,
puts the hat back on.
"Course it'll rain," he says.

Ma says, "Bay,
it hasn't rained enough to grow wheat in
three years."

Daddy looks like a fight brewing.

He takes that red face of his out to the barn,
to keep from feuding with my pregnant ma.
I ask Ma
how, after all this time,
Daddy still believes in rain.

"Well, it rains enough," Ma says,
"now and again,
to keep a person hoping.
But even if it didn't
your daddy would have to believe.
It's coming on spring,
and he's a farmer."

March 1934

MIGRANT MOTHER

Dorothea Lange

Many farm families affected by the Dust Bowl gave up on their land and moved to California. Nicknamed Okies or Arkies because many were from Oklahoma and Arkansas, they packed all of their belongings into a car and traveled hundreds of miles with no guarantee of a job or housing at the end of the journey.

Photographer Dorothea Lange captured many heartbreaking images of these migrant families during her employment with the Farm Security Administration. A photo she took of a young mother at a migrant farm camp in California became one of the most famous images of the 20th century.

Lange gave this account to Popular Photography *magazine in 1960.*

March 1936
Nipomo, California

It was raining, the camera bags were packed, and I had on the seat beside me in the car the results of my long trip, the box containing all those rolls and packs of exposed film ready to mail back to Washington. It was a time of relief. Sixty-five miles an hour for seven hours would get me home to my family that night, and my eyes were glued to the wet and gleaming highway that stretched out ahead. I felt freed, for I could lift my mind off my job and think of home.

I was on my way and barely saw a crude sign with pointing arrow which flashed by at the side of the road, saying PEA-PICKERS CAMP. But out of the corner of my eye I *did* see it.

I didn't want to stop, and didn't. I didn't want to remember that I had seen it, so I drove on and ignored the summons. Then, accompanied by

Left: migrant mother; photo by Dorothea Lange

the rhythmic hum of the windshield wipers, arose an inner argument:

Dorothea, how about that camp back there? What is the situation back there?

Are you going back?

Nobody could ask this of you, now could they?

To turn back certainly is not necessary. Haven't you plenty of negatives already on this subject? Isn't this just one more of the same? Besides, if you take a camera out in this rain, you're just asking for trouble. Now be reasonable, etc., etc., etc.

Having well convinced myself for 20 miles that I could continue on, I did the opposite. Almost without realizing what I was doing I made a U-turn on the empty highway. I went back those 20 miles and turned off the highway at that sign,

PEA-PICKERS CAMP.

I was following instinct, not reason; I drove into that wet and soggy camp and parked my car like a homing pigeon.

I saw and approached the hungry and desperate mother, as if drawn by a magnet. I do not remember how I explained my presence or my camera to her but I do remember she asked me no questions. I made five exposures, working closer and closer from the same direction. I did not ask her name or her history. She told me her age, that she was 32. She said that they had been living on frozen vegetables from the surrounding fields, and birds that the children killed. She had just sold the tires from her car to buy food. There she sat in

that lean-to tent with her children huddled around her, and seemed to know that my pictures might help her, and so she helped me. There was a sort of equality about it.

The pea crop at Nipomo had frozen and there was no work for anybody. But I did not approach the tents and shelters of other stranded pea-pickers. It was not necessary; I knew I had recorded the essence of my assignment. ∾

After returning from the camps, Lange notified a local newspaper editor about the conditions. The federal government sent 20,000 pounds of food to the migrants.

photos by Dorothea Lange

Responding to Cluster Three

How Tough Were the Times?
Thinking Skill ANALYZING

1. In "Digging In" Robert J. Hastings lists a number of items and services his family did without during the Great Depression. Of these, what would be the most difficult for you to give up?

2. What is the **theme** of "The Lesson"?

3. Using the information found in "Black Sunday," "Debts," and "Migrant Mother," **summarize** the effect the Dust Bowl had on farmers.

4. Write a character sketch for the woman pictured in the image "Migrant Mother." Include details about her appearance, her emotions, and how her surroundings seem to affect her.

Writing Activity: Surviving Tough Times

What do you think would happen if one or both of your parents or caretakers lost their jobs and you were living in a period similar to the Great Depression? What might you do to help your family through tough times? **Analyze** your current lifestyle. Then determine the activities and spending habits that are luxuries and those that are essential. Finally, write an essay explaining what actions you would take and sacrifices you would make to save money.

A Strong Analysis

- states the purpose for the analysis
- demonstrates careful examination of each part of the topic
- supports each point with evidence
- organizes information clearly
- ends with a summary of the ideas presented

CLUSTER FOUR

THINKING ON YOUR OWN

Thinking Skill   SYNTHESIZING

DEPRESSION DAYS

PAT MORA

I buy the dark with my last fifteen cents.
Reel after reel, I hide on the decks with men
who fill their chest with salt air of the high seas,
who sing, "Red Sails in the Sunset."

I try not to think of the men who climbed
on the cold truck with me this morning,
stomachs screechy as gears. We were hungry
for paychecks. I try not to think

of last night on my cot, my private reel,
me a border kid, smelling Colorado, gripping an ax,
slicing that cold pine smell, playing CCC lumberjack
in a house dark from my father's death.

Our skin puckered this morning, shrank from the desert
wind that slid into the wooden barracks herding us
around the stove's warm belly, my joke to the doc,
"Am I alive?" limp as the clothes bags around our necks.

I try not to think of the sergeant spitting, *"Delgado,"*
and I step from the line, his glare at my dumbness.
"I said Delgado," me saying, "I am Delgado."
The twitch of his lips. The wind.

Then his "See me later," later trying not to hear
his brand of kindness, "You don't look Mexican, Delgado.
Just change your name and you've got a job."
My father eyeing me.

So I buy the dark with my last fifteen cents.
I try not to think of the bare ice box,[1] my mother's
always sad eyes, of my father who never understood
this country, of the price of eggs and names and skin.

1 **ice box:** a refrigerator that uses large blocks of ice to keep foods cool

THE GOOD PROVIDER

Marion Gross

Minnie Leggety turned up the walk of her Elm Street bungalow and saw that she faced another crisis. When Omar sat brooding like that, not smoking, not "studying," but just scrunched down inside of himself, she knew enough after forty years to realize that she was facing a crisis. As though it weren't enough just trying to get along on Omar's pension these days, without having to baby him through another one of his periods of discouragement! She forced a gaiety into her voice that she actually didn't feel.

"Why, hello there, Pa, what are you doing out here? Did you have to come up for air?" Minnie eased herself down beside Omar on the stoop and put the paper bag she had been carrying on the sidewalk. Such a little bag, but it had taken most of their week's food budget! Protein, plenty of lean, rare steaks and chops, that's what that nice man on the radio said old folks needed, but as long as he couldn't tell you how to buy it with steak at $1.23 a pound, he might just as well save his breath to cool his porridge.[1] And so might she, for all the attention Omar was paying her. He was staring straight ahead as though he didn't even see her. This looked like one of his real bad spells. She took his gnarled hand and patted it.

"What's the matter, Pa? Struck a snag with your gadget?" The "gadget" filled three full walls of the basement and most of the floor space besides, but it was still a "gadget" to Minnie—another one of his ideas that didn't quite work.

---

[1] **save his breath to cool his porridge:** an idiomatic saying meaning he should keep his advice to himself

Omar had been working on gadgets ever since they were married. When they were younger, she hotly sprang to his defense against her sisters-in-law: "Well, it's better than liquor, and it's cheaper than pinochle; at least I know where he is nights." Now that they were older, and Omar was retired from his job, his tinkering took on a new significance. It was what kept him from going to pieces like a lot of men who were retired and didn't have enough activity to fill their time and their minds.

"What's the matter, Pa?" she asked again.

The old man seemed to notice her for the first time. Sadly he shook his head. "Minnie, I'm a failure. The thing's no good; it ain't practical. After all I promised you, Minnie, and the way you stuck by me and all, it's just not going to work."

Minnie never had thought it would. It just didn't seem possible that a body could go gallivanting back and forth the way Pa had said they would if the gadget worked. She continued to pat the hand she held and told him soothingly, "I'm not sure but it's for the best, Pa. I'd sure have gotten airsick, or timesick, or whatever it was. What're you going to work on now that you're giving up the time machine?" she asked anxiously.

"You don't understand, Min," the old man said. "I'm through. I've failed. I've failed at everything I've ever tried to make. They always *almost* work, and yet there's always something I can't get just right. I never knew enough, Min, never had enough schooling, and now it's too late to get any. I'm just giving up altogether. I'm through!"

This *was* serious. Pa with nothing to tinker at down in the basement, Pa constantly underfoot, Pa with nothing to keep him from just slipping away like old Mr. Mason had, was something she didn't like to think about. "Maybe it isn't as bad as all that," she told him. "All those nice parts you put into your gadget, maybe you could make us a television or something with them. Land, a television, that would be a nice thing to have."

"Oh, I couldn't do that, Min. I wouldn't know how to make a television; besides, I told you, it almost works. It's just that it ain't practical. It ain't the way I pictured it. Come down, I'll show you." He dragged her into the house and down into the basement.

The time machine left so little free floor space, what with the furnace and coal bin and washtubs, that Minnie had to stand on the stairway while Pa explained it to her. It needed explanation. It had more colored lights than a pinball machine, more plugs than the Hillsdale telephone exchange, and more levers than one of those newfangled voting booths.

"Now see," he said, pointing to various parts of the machine, "I rigged this thing up so we could move forward or back in time and space both. I thought we could go off and visit foreign spots, and see great things happening, and have ourselves an interesting old age."

"Well, I don't rightly know if I'd have enjoyed that, Pa," Minnie interrupted. "I doubt I'd know how to get along with all them foreigners, and their strange talk and strange ways and all."

Omar shook his head in annoyance. "The Holy Land. You'd have wanted to see the Holy Land, wouldn't you? You could have sat with the crowd at Galilee and listened to the Lord's words right from His lips. You'd have enjoyed that, wouldn't you?"

"Omar, when you talk like that you make the whole thing sound sacrilegious and against the Lord's ways. Besides, I suppose the Lord would have spoke in Hebrew, and I don't know one word of that and you don't either. I don't know but what I'm glad you couldn't get the thing to work," she said righteously.

"But Min, it does work!" Omar was indignant.

"But you said—"

"I never said it don't work. I said it ain't practical. It don't work good enough, and I don't know enough to make it work better."

Working on the gadget was one thing, but believing that it worked was another. Minnie began to be alarmed. Maybe folks had been right— maybe Omar had gone off his head at last. She looked at him anxiously. He seemed all right and, now that he was worked up at her, the depression seemed to have left him.

"What do you mean it works, but not good enough?" she asked him.

"Well, see here," Omar told her, pointing to an elaborate control board. "It was like I was telling you before you interrupted with your not getting along with foreigners, and your sacreligion and all. I set this thing up to move a body in time and space any which way. There's a globe of the world worked in here, and I thought that by turning the globe and setting these time controls to whatever year you had in mind you could go wherever you had a mind to. Well, it don't work like that. I've been trying it out for a whole week and no matter how I set the globe, no matter how I set the time controls, it always comes out the same. It lands me over at Main and Center, right in front of Purdey's meat market."

"What's wrong with that?" Minnie asked. "That might be real convenient."

"You don't understand," Omar told her. "It isn't *now* when I get there, it's twenty years ago! That's the trouble, it don't take me none of the places I want to go, just Main and Center. And it don't take me none of the times I want to go, just twenty years ago, and I saw enough of the depression so I don't want to spend my old age watching people sell apples. Then on top of that, this here timer don't work." He pointed to another dial. "It's supposed to set to how long you want to stay, wherever you want to go, but it don't work at all. Twenty minutes, and then woosh, you're right back here in the basement. Nothing works like I want it to."

Minnie had grown thoughtful as Omar recounted the faults of the machine. Wasn't it a caution[2] the way even a smart man like Pa, a man smart enough to make a time machine, didn't have a practical ounce to his whole hundred and forty-eight pounds. She sat down heavily on the cellar steps and, emptying the contents of her purse on her broad lap, began examining the bills.

"What you looking for, Min?" Omar asked.

Minnie looked at him pityingly. Wasn't it a caution . . .

▲ ▲ ▲

Purdey the butcher was leaning unhappily against his chopping block. The shop was clean and shining, the floor was strewn with fresh sawdust, and Purdey himself, unmindful of the expense, had for the sake of his morale donned a fresh apron. But for all that, Purdey wished that he was hanging on one of his chromium-plated meat hooks.

The sky was blue and smogless, something it never was when the shops were operating and employing the valley's five thousand bread-winners. Such potential customers as were abroad had a shabby, threadbare look to them. Over in front of the Bijou old Mr. Ryan was selling apples.

While he watched, a stout, determined-looking woman appeared at the corner of Main and Center. She glanced quickly around, brushing old Mr. Ryan and his apples with her glance, and then came briskly toward Purdey's shop. Purdey straightened up.

"Afternoon, Ma'am, what can I do for you?" He beamed as though the light bill weren't three months overdue.

2 **a caution:** astonishing

"I'll have a nice porterhouse," the lady said hesitantly. "How much is porterhouse?"

"Forty-five a pound, best in the house." Purdey held up a beauty, expecting her to change her mind.

"I'll take it," the lady said. "And six lamb chops. I want a rib roast for Sunday, but I can come back for that. No use carrying too much," she explained. "Could you please hurry with that? I haven't very much time."

"New in town?" Purdey asked as he turned to ring up the sale on the cash register.

"Yes, you might say so," the woman said. By the time Purdey turned back to ask her name, she was gone. But Purdey knew she'd be back. She wanted a rib roast for Sunday. "It just goes to show you," Purdey said to himself, surveying the satisfactory tab sticking up from the register, "there still is some money around. Two dollars, and she never even batted an eyelash. It goes to show you!" ∾

UPON THE WATERS

JOANNE GREENBERG

It was a bright green day. The big trees on the side streets were raining seeds and the wind stirred in its second sleep. A long flatbed truck
came rattling down Grant Street and stopped by the new steel, chrome,
and glass building. The building's lines were so austere it made Cephas
wonder if anyone really worked in it. Then he saw some women going
in. Good. He checked his appearance by hitching up to the rearview mir-
ror. He was wearing a clean white shirt and a bow tie, and his thin grey
hair had been slicked down with water. When he was sure he was pre-
sentable, he got down out of the cab of the truck, dusted himself off and
began to walk slowly toward the building. It had been many years—perhaps they had moved. No, there was the sign: BOONE COUNTY
DEPARTMENT OF WELFARE. The last time he had been here the building was a temporary shed and the people were lined up outside waiting
for the relief trucks to come. That was in 1934, in the winter. His father
had been proud of holding out till '34. He stopped and looked at the
building again. Some secretaries came out, laughing and talking. They
didn't look at him, being used to seeing people who came hesitantly to
their offices to acknowledge failure in life. Cephas checked himself again
in the big glass door and then went in. There was a large booth with a
woman behind it and eight or nine rows of benches facing it. People
were sitting quietly, staring at nothing, waiting. To the right there were a
series of chutes with numbers over them. Cephas went up to the booth.

"Take a number," the woman said, without looking at him.

"Ma'am?"

"You take a number and wait your turn. We'll call you."

He took one of the plastic number cards. It said 15. He went back, sat down and waited. "Five," the woman called. A heavy woman got up slowly and went to the booth and then to one of the chutes. Cephas waited. Minutes were born, ripened, aged, and died without issue. "Number six." Around him the springtime asthmatics[1] whistled and gasped. He looked at the cracks in his fingers. "Number seven." An hour went by, another. A number, another. He was afraid to go out and check his truck lest the line speed up and he lose his place. "Number thirteen," the woman called.

So they came to his number at last and he went up to the desk, gave back the plastic card and was directed to his chute. Another woman was there at another desk. She took his name, Cephas Ribble, and his age, sixty-eight. Had he been given aid before? Yes. Had he been on General Assistance, Aid to the Needy Disabled? Tuberculosis?

"It was what they called Relief."

"Yes, but under what category was it?"

"It was for the people that was off their farms or else didn't have nothin' to eat. They called it Goin' On The County. It was back in 19 and 34. We held out till '34."

"I see. Now you are applying for the old age pension?" He said he wasn't.

"Are you married, Mr. Ribble?" She sighed. "Never had the pleasure," he said.

"Are you in emergency status?" He said he wasn't.

"All right, then, take this card and go to room 11, on your left." She pressed a little light or something and he felt the people shifting their weight on the benches behind him. Number sixteen, he expected. He made his way to room 11.

The lady there was nice; he could see it right off. She told him about the different kinds of what they call Aid, and then she had him sign some forms: permission to inquire into his bank account, acceptance of surplus or donated food, release of medical information, and several others. Then she said sympathetically, "In what way are you disabled?"

He thought about all the ways a man might be disabled and checked each one off. It was a proud moment, a man sixty-eight without one thing in the world to complain of in his health.

"I ain't disabled no way, but I'm pleased you asked me, though. A man don't take time to be grateful for things like his health. If the shoe don't

---

1 **asthmatics:** individuals who have asthma—a condition often caused by allergies in which sufferers have trouble breathing

pinch, you don't take notice, do you." He sat back, contented. Then he realized that the sun was getting hotter and what with everything in the truck, he'd better get on. The woman had put down her ball point pen. "Mr. Ribble, if you aren't disabled or without funds, what kind of aid do you want?" A shadow of irritation crossed her face.

"No aid at all," he said. "This is about somethin' different." He tried to hold down his excitement. It was his special day, a day for which he had waited for over a decade, but it was no use bragging and playing the boy, so he said no more. The woman was very annoyed. "Then why didn't you tell the worker at the desk?"

"She didn't give me no chance, ma'am, an' neither did that other lady. I bet you don't have many repair men comin' in here to fix things—not above once, anyway."

"Well, Mr. Ribble, what is it you want?" She heard the noise of co-workers leaving and returning from their coffee breaks. She sighed and began to drum her fingers, but he wasn't aware of her impatience. He was beginning back in 1934. She would have to listen to all of it!

"Thirty-four cleaned us out—cleaned us to bone. You wonder how *farmers* could go hungry. I don't know, but we did. After the drought hit there was nothin' to do but come in town an' sign up on the County. Twice a month my pa would come in an' bring back food. Sometimes I came with him. I seen them lines of hungry men just standin' out there like they was poleaxed[2] an' hadn't fallen yet. I tell you, them days was pitiful, *pitiful.*" He glanced up at her and then smiled. "I'm glad to see *you* done good since—got a new buildin' an' all. Yes, you come right up." He looked around with approval at the progress they had made.

"Mr. Ribble . . . ?" He returned. "See, we taken the Relief, but we never got to tell nobody the good it done for us. After that year, things got a little better, and soon we was on toward bein' a payin' farm again. In '46 we built us a new house—every convenience, an' in '56 we got some of them automated units for cattle care. Two years ago we was doin' good, an' last year, I knew it was time to think about My Plan for real. It was time to Thank The Welfare."

"Mr. Ribble, thanks are not necessary. . . ."

"Don't you mind, ma'am, you just get your men an' come with me."

"I beg your pardon. . . ."

"I do more than talk, ma'am. You come on out an' bring your men."

---

2 **poleaxed:** hit with a sharp instrument

Mr. Morrissey had come back from his coffee break and was standing in the hall. She signaled him with her eyes as she followed Cephas Ribble, now walking proud and sure out to his truck. He sighed and followed, wondering why he was always around when somebody needed to make a madness plain. Why did it never happen to McFarland?

Cephas was reaching into his pocket and they thought: *gun*. He took out a piece of paper and turned to them as they stood transfixed and pale and thinking of violence. "I got it all here, all of what's in the truck. Get your men, ma'am; no use wastin' time. It's all in the truck and if it don't get unloaded soon, it's gonna spoil."

"What is this about, Mr. Ribble?"

"My donation, ma'am, I told you. I'm givin' the Relief six hundred chickens, thirty bushels of tomatoes, thirty bushels of apricots—I figured for variety, an' don't you think the apricots was a good idea, though?—ten bushels of beans, six firkins³ of butter—ma'am, you better get them chickens out, it don't do to keep 'em in this sun. I thought about milk, so I give two cans—that's one hundred gallons of milk, you know, for the babies."

They were dumbfounded. Cephas could see that. He wanted to tell them that he wasn't trying to be big. Everybody gives what he can. He's even signed a form right there in the office about promising to accept donated food and clothing. Their amazement at his gift embarrassed him. Then he realized that it was probably the only way they could thank him—by making a fuss. People on the state payroll must have to walk a pretty narrow line. They'd have to be on the lookout for people taking advantage. That was it. It was deep work, that welfare, mighty deep work.

"What are we supposed to do with all that food?" Mr. Morrissey said. Cephas saw that the man was making sure it wasn't a bribe. "Why, give it to the poor. Call 'em in an' let 'em get it. You can have your men unload it right now, an' I'd do it quick if I was you—like I said, it won't be long till it starts to turn in all this heat."

Mr. Morrissey tried to explain that modern welfare methods were different from those of 1934. Even then, the food had been U.S. surplus and not privately donated. It had come from government warehouses. Cephas spoke of the stupidity and waste of Government and rained invective on the Soil Bank and the Department of Agriculture. Mr. Morrissey tried again. "We don't give out any *food*. There hasn't been any *donated* since 1916!"

---

3 **firkins:** casks or small barrels; one firkin is equal to one-fourth barrel

No doubt of it, these welfare people had to be awful careful. Cephas nodded. "The others do what they can—don't blame 'em if it don't seem like much," he said sympathetically. "I signed that slip in there about the donated food, so there must *be* some donated."

"It's done because of an obsolete law," Mrs. Traphagen argued, "one of the old Poor Laws that never got taken off the books."

"—an' here you folks are followin' it, right today," Cephas mused, "it must make you mighty proud."

"Mr. Ribble, *we have no place to store all this!*"

Cephas found his throat tightening with happiness. He had come in humility, waited all the morning just so he could show his small gratitude and be gone, and here were these people thunderstruck at the plenty. "Mister," he said, "I pay my taxes without complainin', but I never knowed how hard you people was workin' for your money. You got to guard against every kind of bribes and invitations to break the law; you got to find ways to get this food to the poor people so fast, you can't even store it! Mister, you make me proud to be an American!"

A policeman had stopped by the truck and was tranquilly writing a ticket. Cephas excused himself modestly and strode off to defend his situation. The two workers stood staring after him as he engaged the officer. It was, after all, state law that food could be donated. Had the department no parking place for donors? The policeman looked over at the stunned bearers of the state's trust. He had stopped writing.

"Could that truck fit in the workers' parking lot?" Morrissey murmured.

"What are we going to do with it all?" whimpered Mrs. Traphagen.

"All those chickens—six hundred chickens!"

"The poor will never stand for it," Mrs. Traphagen sighed.

"First things first," Mr. Morrissey decided, and went to confront the policeman.

Cephas's truck in the workers' parking lot blocked all their cars. As a consequence, the aid applications of eight families were held pending investigation. Six discharged inmates of the state hospital remained incarcerated for a week longer pending home checkups. Thirty-seven women washed floors and children's faces in the expectation of home visits which were not made. A meeting on disease at the Midtown Hotel was one speaker short, and high school students scheduled to hear Social Work, Career of Tomorrow, remained unedified. Applicants who came to apply for aid that afternoon were turned away. There was no trade in little plastic cards and the hive of offices was empty. But the people of the

Boone County Department of Public Welfare were not idle. It was only that the action had moved from the desks and files and chutes to the workers' parking lot and into the hands of its glad tyrant, Cephas Ribble.

All afternoon Cephas lifted huge baskets of apricots and tomatoes into the arms of the welfare workers. All afternoon they went from his truck to their cars carrying the baskets, chickens festooned[4] limply over their arms. When they complained to Mr. Morrissey, he waved them off. Were they to go to every home and deliver the food, they asked? Were big families to get the same amount as small families?

Cephas was a titan.[5] He lifted smiling, and loaded with a strong arm. He never stopped for rest or to take a drink. The truck steamed in the hot spring light, but he was living at height,[6] unbothered by the heat or the closeness or the increasing rankness of his chickens. Of course he saw that the welfare people weren't dressed for unloading food. They were dressed for church, looked like. It was deep work, very deep, working for the state. You had to set a good example. You had to dress up and talk very educated so as to give the poor a moral uplift.

You had to be honest. A poor man could lie—he'd been poor himself so he knew, but it must be a torment to deal with people free to lie and not be able to do it yourself.

By 3:30 the truck had been unloaded into the cars and Cephas was free to go home and take up his daily life again. He shook hands with the director and the casework supervisor, the head bookkeeper and the statistician. To them he presented his itemized list, carefully weighed and given the market value as of yesterday, in case they needed it for their records. Then he carefully turned the truck out of the parking lot, waved goodbye to the sweating group, nosed into the sluggish mass of afternoon traffic and began to head home. The lot burst into a cacophony of high-pitched voices:

"I've got three mothers of dropouts to visit!"

"What am I going to *do* with all this stuff?"

"Who do we give this to? My people won't take the Lady Bountiful bit!"

"Does it count on their food allowance? Do we go down Vandalia and hand out apricots to every kid we see?"

"I don't have the time!"

"Which families get it?"

---

4 **festooned:** hung decoratively

5 **titan:** a giant

6 **living at height:** incredibly happy

"Do we take the value off next month's check?"

"It's hopeless to try to distribute this fairly," the supervisor said.

"It will cost us close to a thousand dollars to distribute it at all," the statistician said.

"It would cost us close to two thousand to alter next month's checks," the bookkeeper said, "and the law specifies that we have to take extra income-in-kind off the monthly allowance."

"If I were you," Morrissey said, "I would take all this home and eat it and not let anyone know about it."

"Mr. Morrissey!" Mrs. Traphagen's face paled away the red of her exertion. "That is fraud! You know as well as I do what would happen if it got out that we had diverted welfare commodities[7] to our own use! Can you imagine what the mayor would say, what the governor would say, the state legislature, the Department of Health, Education, and Welfare, the National Association of Social Workers!" She had begun to tremble and the two chickens that were hanging over her arm nodded to one another, with a kind of slow decorum, their eyes closed righteously against the thought. Motors started, horns sounded and cars began to clot the exit of the parking lot. The air was redolent.

As the afternoon wore on, apricots began to appear in the hands of children from Sixteenth and Vandalia Street all the way to the Boulevard. Tomatoes flamed briefly on the windowsills of the ghetto between Fourteenth and Kirk, and on one block, there was a chicken in every pot.

The complaints began early the next day. Sixteen people called the Mayor's Committee on Discrimination claiming that chickens, fruit, and vegetables had been given to others while they had received tomatoes, half of them rotten. A rumor began that the food had been impregnated with medicine to test on the poor and that three people had died from it. The Health Department finally issued a denial, which brought a score of reporters to its door. During the questioning by reporters, a chemist at the department called the whole affair "the blatherings of a bunch of pinheads on the lunatic fringe." On the following day, the department received complaints from the ACLU, the Black Muslims, and the Diocesan Council,[8] all of whom demanded apologies. There were eighteen calls at the Department of Welfare protesting a tomato "bombing"

---

7 **commodities:** goods

8 **ACLU, the Black Muslims, and the Diocesan Council:** all are groups with political agendas concerning the underprivileged. ACLU is short for the American Civil Liberties Union.

which had taken place on Fourteenth and Vandalia, in which passersby had been hit with tomatoes dropped from the roofs of slum houses. The callers demanded that the families of those involved be stricken from the welfare rolls as relief cheaters, encouraging waste and damaging the moral fiber of the young. Twenty-two mothers on the Aid to Dependent Children program picketed the governor's mansion carrying placards saying *Hope, Not Handouts* and *Jobs, Not Charity*. Sixty-eight welfare clients called to say that they had received no food at all and demanded equal service. When they heard that the Vandalia Street mothers were picketing, a group of them went down to protest. Words were exchanged between the two groups and a riot ensued in which sixteen people were hospitalized for injuries, including six members of the city's riot squad. Seven of the leaders and four who were bystanders were jailed pending investigation. The FBI was called into the case in the evening to ascertain if the riot was Communist-inspired. At ten o'clock, the mayor went on TV with a plea for reason and patience. He stated that the riot was a reflection of the general decline in American morals and a lack of respect for the law. He ordered a six-man commission to be set up to hear testimony and make recommendations. A political opponent demanded a thorough investigation of the county welfare system and the local university's hippies. On the following day, Mrs. Traphagen was unable to go to work at the welfare office, having been badly scalded on the hand while canning a bushel of apricots.

Cephas Ribble remembered everyone at the welfare office in his prayers. After work he would think about the day he had spent in the city and of his various triumphs. The surprise and wonder on the faces of the workers, and the modest awe of the woman who had said, "Mr. Ribble, you don't need to thank us," humbled and moved him. It had been a wonderful day. He had given his plenty unto the poor, plenty that was the doing of his own hands. He rose refreshed into his work, marveling at the meaning and grandeur in which his simplest chores were suddenly invested. He said, as he checked his chickens, "A man has his good to do. I'm gonna do it every year. I'm gonna have a day for the poor. Yessir, every year!" and he smiled genially on the chickens, the outbuildings, and the ripening fields of a generous land. ஊ

A Touch of Rue

Virginia Durr and Studs Terkel

Wetumpka, Alabama. It is an old family house on the outskirts of Montgomery. A creek runs by. . . . She and her husband, Clifford, are of an old Alabamian lineage. During Franklin Roosevelt's administration, he was a member of the Federal Communications Commission. She had been a pioneer in the battle to abolish the poll tax.

Oh, no, the Depression was not a romantic time. It was a time of terrible suffering. The contradictions were so obvious that it didn't take a very bright person to realize something was terribly wrong.

Have you ever seen a child with rickets? Shaking as with palsy.[1] No proteins, no milk. And the companies pouring milk into gutters. People with nothing to wear, and they were plowing up cotton. People with nothing to eat, and they killed the pigs. If that wasn't the craziest system in the world, could you imagine anything more idiotic? This was just insane.

And people blamed themselves, not the system. They felt they had been at fault: . . . "if we hadn't bought that old radio" . . . "if we hadn't bought that old secondhand car." Among the things that horrified me were the preachers—the fundamentalists. They would tell the people they suffered because of their sins. And the people believed it. God was punishing them. Their children were starving because of their sins.

People who were independent, who thought they were masters and mistresses of their lives, were all of a sudden dependent on others.

---

1 **rickets...palsy:** Rickets is a disease affecting young children, in which the bones become deformed from a lack of calcium and vitamin D; palsy is a condition marked by tremors or shaking of the body.

Relatives or relief. People of pride went into shock and sanitoriums. My mother was one.

Up to this time, I had been a conformist, a Southern snob. I actually thought the only people who amounted to anything were the very small group which I belonged to. The fact that my family wasn't as well off as those of the girls I went with—I was vice president of Junior League— made me value even more the idea of being well-born. . . .

What I learned during the Depression changed all that. I saw a blinding light like Saul on the road to Damascus.[2] (Laughs.) It was the first time I had seen the other side of the tracks. The rickets, the pellagra[3]—it shook me up. I saw the world as it really was.

She shamed, cajoled and persuaded the dairy company into opening milk dispensaries. When they sought to back down, she convinced them that "if these people got a taste of milk, they might get in the habit of buying it— when they got jobs."

When the steel companies closed down in Birmingham, thousands were thrown out of work. She was acquainted with some of the executives; she argued with them: "You feed the mules who work in your mines. Why don't you feed the people? You're responsible."

The young today are just play-acting in courting poverty. It's all right to wear jeans and eat hamburgers. But it's entirely different from not having any hamburgers to eat and no jeans to wear. A great many of these kids—white kids—seem to have somebody in the background they can always go to. I admire their spirit, because they have a strong sense of social justice. But they themselves have not been deprived. They haven't experienced the terror. They have never seen a baby in the cradle crying of hunger. . . .

I think the reason for the gap between the black militants and the young white radicals[4] is that the black kids are much more conscious

2 **a blinding light like Saul on the road to Damascus:** The story of Saul is told in the New Testament. He was a religious zealot who persecuted Christians until he had a mystical encounter with Christ on the road to Damascus. He then changed his name to Paul and became a Christian missionary

3 **pellagra:** a disease of the stomach and nervous system, caused by a lack of niacin

4 **black militants... white radicals:** a reference to groups who worked for social change during the 1960's and 70's

of the thin edge of poverty. And how soon you can be reduced to living on relief. What you *know* and what you *feel* are very different. Terror is something you *feel*. When there is no paycheck coming in—the absolute, stark terror.

What frightens me is that these kids are like sheep being lead to slaughter. They are romantic and they are young. I have a great deal more faith in movements that start from necessity—people trying to change things because of their own deprivation. We felt that in the labor surge of the Thirties. The people who worked hardest to organize were the ones in the shops and in the mills.

The Depression affected people in two different ways. The great majority reacted by thinking money is the most important thing in the world. Get yours. And get it for your children. Nothing else matters. Not having that stark terror come at you again. . . .

And there was a small number of people who felt that the whole system was lousy. You have to change it. The kids come along and they want to change it, too. But they don't seem to know what to put in its place. I'm not so sure I know, either. I do think it has to be responsive to people's needs. And it has to be done by democratic means, if possible. Whether it's possible or not—the power of money is such today, I just don't know. Some of the kids call me a relic of the Thirties. Well, I am. ∾

RESPONDING TO CLUSTER FOUR

Thinking Skill   SYNTHESIZING

1. Each of the other clusters in this book is introduced by a question that is meant to help readers focus their thinking about the selections. What do you think the question for cluster four should be?

2. How do you think the selections in this cluster should be taught? Demonstrate your ideas by joining with your classmates to: a) create discussion questions b) lead discussions about the selections c) develop vocabulary quizzes d) prepare a cluster quiz

REFLECTING ON DARK DAYS

Essential Question   WHAT WAS THE GREAT DEPRESSION?

Reflecting on this book as a whole provides an opportunity for independent learning and the application of the critical thinking skill, synthesis. *Synthesizing* means examining all the things you have learned from this book and combining them to form a richer and more meaningful view of the Depression's impact on American society.

There are many ways to demonstrate what you know about the Great Depression. Here are some possibilities. Your teacher may provide others.

1. After reading this book, you should have a better understanding of the effect the Great Depression has had on America's history. Write an essay that synthesizes what you have learned about the Great Depression and its effects on the people who lived through it, as well as its effects on our modern-day life.

2. Individually or in small groups, develop an independent project that demonstrates your knowledge of The Great Depression. For example, you might create your own documentary on the Great Depression in your town Other options might include a music video, dance, poem, performance, drama, or artistic rendering.

3. The Great Depression changed the way people viewed America and themselves. The government began to play a larger role in peoples' lives, first through relief efforts, then through programs such as Social Security, the Tennessee Valley Authority, and the Securities and Exchange Commission. Some people today believe that as a result, the government is too involved in our lives, others believe the government should be more involved, and some programs, such as the Civilian Conservation Corps, should be resurrected. Stage a debate on one of the following issues.

   Resolved: The United States Government should end Depression-era programs, such as Social Security and the Federal Deposit Insurance Corporation.

   Resolved: The Great Depression was good for the United States.

Acknowledgments

Text Credits CONTINUED FROM PAGE 2 "Letters to the Roosevelts" from *Down and Out in the Great Depression: Letters from the Forgotten Man* by Robert S. McElvaine. Copyright © 1983 by the University of North Carolina Press. Used by permission of the publisher.

"The Lesson" by Harry Mark Petrakis. Reprinted from *Tales of the Heart, Dreams and Memories of a Lifetime*, 1999. Copyright Harry Mark Petrakis.

"Migrant Mother" by Dorothea Lange. Copyright the Dorothea Lange Collection, the Oakland Museum of California, City of Oakland. Gift of Paul S. Taylor.

"A One-Woman Crime Wave", from *A Long Way from Chicago* by Richard Peck, copyright © 1998 by Richard Peck. Used by permission of Dial Books for Young Readers, a division of Penguin Putnam Inc.

"The Song" from *Hard Times* by Studs Terkel. Copyright © 1970, 1986 by Studs Terkel. Reprinted by permission of Pantheon Books, a division of Random House, Inc.

"A Touch of Rue" by Virginia Durr, from *Hard Times: An Oral History of the Great Depression* by Studs Terkel. Copyright © 1970 by Studs Terkel. Reprinted by permission of Pantheon Books, a division of Random House, Inc.

"Upon the Waters" from *Rites of Passage* by Joanne Greenberg. Copyright © 1972 by Joanne Greenberg. Permission granted by the Wallace Literary Agency, Inc.

"Voices of Discontent" by Gail Stewart, from *The New Deal* (1993). Reprinted by permission of the author.

Every reasonable effort has been made to properly acknowledge ownership of all material used. Any omissions or mistakes are not intentional and, if brought to the publisher's attention, will be corrected in future editions.